LOVE, LIVE AND LEAP AHEAD

LOVE, LIVE AND LEAP AHEAD

QAMRUDDIN

PARTRIDGE

A Penguin Random House Company

To order additional copies of this book, contact
Partridge India
000 800 10062 62
orders.india@partridgepublishing.com

www.partridgepublishing.com/india

CONTENTS

Words from author of the book vii
Acknowledgement...ix
Chapter 1 1
Chapter 2 9
Chapter 3 17
Chapter 4 30
Chapter 5 35
Chapter 6 42
Chapter 7 47
Chapter 8 55
Chapter 9 62
Chapter 10 74
Chapter 11 80
Chapter 12 92
Chapter 13 99
Chapter 14 105
Chapter 15 111
Chapter 16 115
Chapter 17 122
Chapter 18 133
Chapter 19 143
Chapter 20 148
Chapter 21 159
Chapter 22 163
Chapter 23 172
Chapter 24 184
Chapter 25 200
Chapter 26 204
Chapter 27 206

WORDS FROM AUTHOR OF THE BOOK

We are desperately in need of hope, courage, serenity, faith, peace of mind and gratitude for Almighty. I have weaved together motivational success principles in story form in this book to inspire you in day-to-day life.

You may categorize this book as a fiction or a motivational book, whatever you like. But for me it is a motivational fiction. This book, 'Love, Live and Leap Ahead' tells us how to put the great ideology into practice in day-to-day mundane life.

I have intertwined the ideas in the story form in this book to generate curiosity. This is an amazing fiction, incorporating principles of success, happiness, joy and human spirituality and built on insights into unconditional love, forgiveness, gratitude, understanding, enthusiasm, hope and faith.

This motivational fiction demonstrates how you can be happy, serene and successful in all the circumstances. This is a journey into your subconscious mind. Just read it for the joy of reading and let the subconscious take over and ingrain success principles and inspirational ideas into your disposition.

ACKNOWLEDGEMENT

First and foremost, I am thankful to you, dear readers. Without your love for my writings, my efforts would have become useless. I want to be loved by you, not admired, as love is permanent and admiration is transitory.

I am thankful to my family members for faith, love, support, patience and encouragement. I would also like to thank Khadija, my wife, and Hafiza, my mother for creating conducive environment, in which I could let my creative juice flow. My family members continue to support me in all my ventures. They helped me with their time and various practical ideas.

I specially thank my elder son, Mohammed Shaz Qamar, himself a great writer of his famous book, 'You Look Fit'. He and Farzana, my daughter-in-law have helped me with so many practical ideas and time. They inspired me to keep going when going was tough.

Mohammed Shiraz Qamar, my younger son, himself a world famous writer of a famous book, 'Mind Your Intellect', has given his valuable time, suggestions and ideas to complete this book. He constantly reviews all my writings, recordings and works. He has been a great inspiration to me for writing this and a few more other books. He has helped me in editing this book, designing cover and giving this book a presentable shape.

I am, especially, thankful to Meetakshi. She has given ample time to review and edit this book. Her perspicacious analysis helped me improve presentation style, flow and pattern of the book.

I am thankful to my friends and colleagues who have been constant source of inspiration to me in this venture and they have given maximum support, time and motivation for completing this book. I am thankful to my publisher, Partridge India, and all those who have been connected with me in this endeavor.

CHAPTER 1

Manish relishes the memory of the day he met Pushpanjali for the first time. Coming from his office one day in the evening, he noticed a car moving ahead of him gradually stopped with some jerks. The car was being driven by a beautiful young lady. Being a helpful person by nature, he also stopped the car on the side of the road. The young lady in the car ahead was a bit upset for unexpected problem in the car. He offered for help and asked, "May I help you young lady?"

"Thank you very much for your concern," responded the lady. She was happy that someone was there to extend helping hand in that situation. "I think some snag has developed in the car. It has stopped after a few jerks. I do not know much about the car."

"Yes, I too noticed. Do not worry and take it easy. May be I can help you and fix the problem, if it is not enormous. Just relax. I am sure, I will be able to do something."

Both got down their cars. Manish opened the bonnet of the car. It did not take him much time to find out the problem. A wire connection was loose. He tightened it and the problem was so easily over.

"Please start the car now, I hope the problem is over," said Manish cleaning his hand with a cloth. She tried and the car started easily. She felt relieved.

"Yes everything is now ok. Now I feel free from stress and relieved. Thank you very much. You are so helpful. My name is Pushpanjali, by the way," she grinned, beaming with joy extending her hand.

"It is my pleasure . . . I am Manish," reciprocated Manish with soft voice and shook hands. "Pushpanjali, you should be so strong that such minor inconveniences should never disturb your peace of mind. Everybody encounters approximately 23 minor disappointments every day. If you encounter less than that you are lucky. Here is my visiting card. It will be my pleasure, if I can be of any help in future."

"My house is nearby, only 3 minutes' drive. We may have coffee, if you do not mind. My parents will also be happy to meet you."

"Thank you very much Pushpanjali. Today I am a bit in hurry. I have to rush to a nearby hospital just now. We will meet some other day, very soon, at an earliest opportunity. Please keep in touch. I have given you my card. My Facebook ID is also there." said Manish amicably. "You may call me any time."

"Yes, I will be glad to communicate with you soon again," affirmed Pushpanjali reassuringly.

"Thanks."

"Why are you going to hospital? Is everything alright? May I help you?" asked Pushpanjali with concern.

"It is okay . . . thanks . . . There is nothing to worry. I have to see my aunt in the hospital. She is a great social worker in our area. Her ex-husband has donated bone marrow 9 times to help treat her cancer. He communicates directly to her doctor and does it without telling when he has an appointment."

"Is she improving," she said with concern.

"Yes, to a great extent. The treatment appears to be working as the Cancer cells have been drastically reduced recently. He is also visiting hospital today and I will have an opportunity to meet that great soul. Both are great inspiration to me. They are both going to remarry after 10 years of divorce."

"Wow, interesting. I am impressed. I will also like to meet them some day," squeaked Pushpanjali. "Take care . . . see you . . . Bye for now Manish."

"Bye."

One day he was on Facebook. He noticed friendship invitation from Pushpanjali. He clicked for acceptance. She was present and started chat with him after expressing thanks for acceptance of the request.

"Hi, Pushpanjali, I am glad to see you on the Facebook so early in the morning," typed Manish. "In fact I was thinking about you."

"Really? Same here." I was also thinking about you.

"Law of Attraction always works."

"What is this 'Law of Attraction'? I have never heard of it." asked Pushpanjali.

"Let us discuss something else. We are communicating for the first time after meeting that day."

"No, I am interested. You have to explain it now," she insisted with childlike curiosity. "I like such topics."

"Ok, I explain. 'Law of Attraction' says that you attract into your life, whatever you passionately think and feel about. You can get anything you like, provided you desire it badly enough." typed Manish.

He started the web cam and sent her request, "Let us start the web cam."

"Can you hear me?" she asked curiously on the web cam with head phone. She appeared eager to know more about 'Law of Attraction'."

"Yes Pushpanjali, I can, very well, hear you and see your cute smile too," said he joyously. "Decide what you want to attract in your life and write it down. You should see your goals specifically, till they become your second nature."

"Does it really work?"

"'Law of Attraction' is as true as 'Law of Gravity' and other tested universal laws. According to it, if you have a passionate desire to achieve something, you will certainly get it. Decide what you want and release it to universe."

"Interesting, indeed."

"Is there some time limit for delivery?"

"The universe will plan to deliver it to you in its own way. It will deliver it in its own time, when time is ripe for its delivery."

"Pre-mature delivery is problematic," whispered Manish with a smile. "The great Genie or Universe always says one thing, 'your wish is my command.' Give your pure thought to it and affirm continuously, then your subconscious will take over and the universe will deliver it to you in the appropriate time."

"Wow, great," said Pushpanjali smiling. "I like the way you eloquently express your ideas with touch of humor. It is interesting to talk to you. I wish I should have met you earlier. Where have you been for all these years? How can I make it more effective?"

"Thanks Pushpanjali . . . Passionate desires and pure thoughts create environment for positive results," he added.

"How we can create such an environment?"

"De-clutter your mind and remove negative thoughts," said Manish. "Then you may pray, trust, express your gratitude to God in advance and receive."

"Is it the proper way to start?"

"No," said Manish. "Start with deep breathing. Meditate for 10 to 15 minutes. Doing this will relax your mind and you will be in the receptive mode," said Manish.

"I am not expert in deep breathing and meditation," said Pushpanjali.

"That I will tell you in detail, when we meet," said Manish. "When you are relaxed, in pre-sleep or Alfa stage, decide what you want. Be sure it is something you have strong passion for. It should be in conformity with your cherished vision."

"After that?"

"It will be better to write your wish down and send request to the universe. Write it in the present tense. Imagine your desire is already fulfilled and be grateful to God for it," expatiated Manish.

"How will my desires be fulfilled and which time?" asked Pushpanjali. "Will I have to wait for a long time?"

"You appear to be desperate. Desperation is negative and it never works. Passionate desire is positive. That is what you require to have," said Manish. "Manifestation is not your job, but the job of the universe. Trust the universe and be patient. Don't worry about the 'how' of things. Let the universe do it for you."

He paused for a while, appeared concerned and said, "I hope I am not boring you Pushpanjali."

"No dear. I am learning as well as enjoying. Continue please. What other steps should one take?" she asked, eager to know more in detail. Sometimes I forget things to do. How can I get rid of this problem?

"You should prepare comprehensive list of things-to-do and paste it at a place where you can see time to time. The better option for keeping important things in constantly in mind is to prepare a vision board."

"What is vision board?"

"It is a board where you can paste colorful cuttings, text, images of the things you are passionate about. Vision board helps you see, visualize and feel what you want. Look at that picture every day and feel, as feeling is the most important step for manifestation. If you want to attract an experience or an event that makes you joyful and delighted, then keep in mind your feeling and inner emotion. Do not just think about what you want, but visualize and feel it."

"How can I visualize and feel? Can you explain more in detail?"

"You might have experienced some euphoric moments in your life. Recall sports events or happy occasions which gave you immense joy. Recall how you were applauded. Order that feeling in the present activity."

"Very interesting indeed," she quipped with refreshing simplicity. "What to avoid? I mean tell me something about negative blockages."

"The universe does not recognize negatives. Focus as often as possible, on what you do want, rather than on what you do not want."

"Okay."

"If your current reality is bad, try not to think too much about it. If you are constantly worried about bad things happening, or negative outcomes, then you are using the law of attraction against yourself."

"Is thinking or feeling more important?"

"Feelings are more important. If you want something to happen, such as, you want a car; don't just say that you want that car, feel and believe that you are going to get that car and envision yourself riding that car and express your gratitude to God in advance."

"How will I know that it works?" asked Pushpanjali. "I mean, how I will know that I am on the right track?"

"The only way you will know if this works is to try it out for yourself. In the meantime believe that it works. Be optimist, a tough-minded optimist," affirmed Manish convincingly. "Have unlimited enthusiasm and faith."

"This is all very interesting indeed. I feel motivated. Thanks for giving your valuable time telling me in detail."

"It requires lot of time. We will discuss in detail when we meet. In the meantime imagine and feel that you already have what you want; let the feelings of joy, satisfaction, fulfillment, etc. wash over you.

Go about each day relaxed and confident, assured that your desire is on its way to you. Your dominant thoughts and feelings will find a way to manifest," added Manish.

"Great, thanks for your valuable suggestions. We will discuss more about this topic when we meet. I am eager to know more about you," murmured Pushpanjali with charming smile and twinkle in her eyes.

"Then we will meet soon and discuss more about each other. Let us meet tomorrow at Minerva resort in the evening," said Pushpanjali with glow in her eyes. "I will be there at 7.30 in the evening. Will this time suit you?"

"Yes."

CHAPTER 2

When Manish got up in the morning, he expressed his gratitude to God for waking up alive, energetic and healthy. He meditated and practiced deep breathing for 20 minutes and relaxed. He visualized nice day ahead and set intentions for the day. He took a few relaxing deep breaths. He blessed everything and everyone.

He never forgot three things for starting the day. Firstly he set intentions of the day. Then visualized nice day ahead and then went for gratitude walk. He expressed gratitude and blessed everyone and everything at every step. This was his usual way of starting the day with gratitude.

It was his usual practice to look into the mirror and he always appreciated what he saw in it. Today also he stood in front of mirror and said smiling looking into his eyes in the mirror, *"Good morning Mr. Manish. I woke up alive and healthy today. Thank you very much God for giving me another beautiful day, full of joy, health, vigor and contentment. I have so many amenities in my life which many people want to have, but unfortunately they do not have. Thank you God for keeping me free from so many problems. This is an exquisite and wonderful day you have made it. With your help I am going to make it beautiful day by working smartly and visualizing nice things ahead."* He said enthusiastically, feeling every word.

He sat in the veranda and listened to motivational clips in his I-Pod. He visualized nice day ahead, meeting his clients in Hotel Ashok and have meaningful interactions to persuade them to attend his training course.

He also visualized meeting Pushpanjali later in the evening and have a wonderful time with her. Whenever he thought about Pushpanjali, he always felt immense joy and rush of blood in his veins.

Manish reached there at 7.30 and waited outside the restaurant. She also reached after 10 minutes.

"Sorry I kept you waiting. I am 10 minutes late," said Pushpanjali. "There was traffic congestion and it took more time in parking."

"It is okay. I did not have to wait much. Should we go inside?"

"Yes."

Manish was feeling glad to meet her today in the restaurant. Body language of both of them revealed that they were both immensely delighted. Manish cast sweeping glance over her frame, features and face and caught her eyes. She had strange feelings to notice that she was being noticed and appreciated. This feeling enhanced her self-esteem. She looked great in pink sari. Most of the time she appeared amused and retained joyful demeanor.

Restaurant was a bit crowded, but had a joyful ambience. It was a great happening place with lot of bustle. Young couples were in search of solitary corners which were missing. They appeared to be least interested in gastronomic delights. People were enjoying and making best of their time. They managed to get seats in a solitary place.

"It is a nice place to meet. Have you been here earlier?" asked Manish.

"Yes, three times earlier; I came here with my sister Parinita."

"Parinita? Name appears to be familiar. Probably I had heard this name earlier," said Manish. "I am eager to know about you. Tell me what you do and what your hobbies are?

"I belong to a middle class family. I was born and brought up in this city, Delhi. I have mother, father and a sister in my family," said Pushpanjali. "Public speaking, playing Table Tennis, dancing and reading are my main hobbies. My father is a business man and sister is preparing for engineering entrance exam. I am preparing for civil services exam. I am also eager to know about you."

I was also born and brought up like you in Delhi. I have a brother, father and mother. My father has got his own business," said Manish. "I have done my post-graduation in English. I am a voracious reader and reading is my main hobby. I am a motivational trainer, speaker and a life coach. Badminton is my favorite game. My brother is doing preparation for engineering entrance examination."

"I have told you about my present work and hobbies and future aspirations. I have yet tell about my past."

"I do not think that is important. We should live only in the present moment. Should not we?"

"You are correct, but do not you think that past is also useful and helps us in various ways? We get valuable lessons from our past mistakes, if you analyze them with a positive mental attitude and take a lesson. What we are today, depends on our past attitudes, feelings, actions and thoughts."

"You are correct and I agree too, but you will also agree that our dwelling place should be in the present moment. We may, however, visit for a short time, past for learning lessons from mistakes and future for planning course of action."

"I was eager to meet you. I am happy I got the opportunity to meet you today."

"Why, what is so special in me?" asked Pushpanjali with enticing grin. "I am a modest person with simple lifestyle."

"You have a charming and lovely face and wonderful smile." said Manish looking into her eyes with an innocent smile. Noticing uneasy feelings on her face, he changed the topic. "Tell me about your hobbies."

"I have great appetite for learning from all sources. Reading is my main hobby. I have good knowledge of various subjects . . ." said Pushpanjali looking into his eyes with alluring glance.

". . . . and a sound mind in a beautiful body. You have many assets, many people do not have. You are a unique creation of God," chuckled Manish laughingly, looking into her eyes and completed her sentence. He surveyed her face with his constant gaze and realized that she has beautiful and expressive face. She has alluring smile. "You have the most captivating smile I have ever noticed on anyone else's face. When you smile, your eyes also smile."

"*You are handsome and irresistible,*" she wanted to say but could not. Blushing furiously she managed tentative smile in return.

"Do you want to say something?"

"Nothing," said Pushpanjali with twinkle in her eyes. "I hope you are not flirting with me, are you?"

"Not at all."

"I am a practical psychologist. I bet, I can tell you any time, what is going on in your mind," quipped Pushpanjali with a wicked grin. "I can also find out whether you are sincerely appreciating or flirting. Always be careful, especially while looking into my eyes."

"Do not you feel you are lovely?" asked Manish with amusement. "You are finest creation of Almighty. There has been, is or will be no one like you in this world dear. I hope you do not mind mentioning you 'dear'."

"*You can mention even sweetie, honey . . . darling . . .*" she thought but mumbled, "As you like. We are a close friend."

"Yes, I am. I believe and feel so," quipped Manish. What is secret behind your attractive personality?"

"I strongly believe that first step looking best about myself is feeling best about myself. I have requisite self-confidence and self-esteem which further enhances my splendor," chuckled Pushpanjali with an alluring smile.

"Your dressing sense and choice of dress is also superb. You take care to dress to the occasion. You are irresistible."

"Uff . . . Manish . . . it is too much. Let me first digest it," said she with a smile.

"Please do not misunderstand me dear, I appreciate, assess and value only real assets. We must be grateful to God for his finest blessings. You are loveable, loving and cute. Grace and self-confidence makes you stand out. I am really proud to be your friend," said Manish smiling. "I wish, I should have met you earlier. I feel very happy and comfortable in your company."

"I am also glad we met that day darling. You are a nice friend. God plans everything in His own way. He wanted us to meet, so we met. God gives us everything in His own time when time is ripe. That day God disconnected a wire in my car to establish connection between you and me," quipped Pushpanjali smiling.

"Now I have to ask Him what are His other plans. He has sent us in this world and He is always here to help and guide us. He never leaves us alone," quipped Manish laughingly. "Now I remember where I heard name Parinita. My brother Himanshu mentioned it."

"Wow, is Himanshu your brother? Parinita also mentioned about him. What a pleasant surprise! They are close friends. They often meet for preparation and study together."

"I am glad to know that they are friends. There are so many pleasant surprises. We have to find out, if our parents are also acquainted with each other."

"You never know, this may also happen. They are old residents of Delhi. What is name of your father? I will discuss about him with my father."

"His name is Pramod. Should we move now?" said Manish, holding her hand in his hand. "When am I going to see this beautiful smiling face again? I feel very happy in your company."

"I also feel ecstatic to be with you and talk to you dear Manish. Tomorrow I have to go to a college for a presentation. I wish you also spare some time to accompany me to the venue. Your presence will mean a lot to me."

"Why not dear? I am not a fool to miss this opportunity to share beautiful moments with you," chuckled Manish. "I feel great to interact with you and meet you."

"I also feel blissful when I am with you."

"Should I come to your house and pick you up?" Manish offered cheerfully.

"No, instead, I will pick you up at 9, morning on my way to my venue of presentation. I want some tips, tools and techniques for effective and powerful presentation. I have to prepare it today. Can you give me some tips, tools and techniques for preparation?" asked Pushpanjali. "I have requisite confidence to speak in public, but I want to sharpen my tools further and I deliver presentation with power, passion and professionalism."

"Yes dear. Preparation is very important. You must prepare thoroughly and comprehensively, but do not over prepare. Do not forget importance of rehearsal to speak with power, purpose and professionalism. Rehearse, rehearse, and rehearse."

"Nice suggestion dear, thanks."

"Remember to keep your speech simple and to the point. People have tendency to remember only three things. Find 3 most important points you want to convey to your audience and expand these three points for conveying effectively," expounded Manish. "I think this is enough for today. Remaining things we will discuss in the car tomorrow."

"Thanks Manish for nice suggestions. Thank you very much for your beautiful company," she beamed joyfully, looking straight into his eyes. "I shall always relish the reminiscences of beautiful moments shared with you."

"Yes dear, we had great time together. Keep in touch on phone and social media when you do not have much time to meet. Let me accompany you up to your car," He offered with alacrity.

"Do not bother dear, I will manage," said she with an alluring grin and measure of conviction in her voice. "You have done too much. That is sufficient for today. Bye darling, take care."

"Bye sweetie."

CHAPTER 3

He had awakened with strange feeling of being in a hurry and wanting to be soon with Pushpanjali. He always had same feeling whenever he fixed to meet her. He was ready when she reached his residence. She was looking extremely beautiful in light orange sari and matching blouse. Matching orange lipstick was creating magic. He was surprised about her choice of dresses. Most of the time she was putting on dresses of his choice.

"*How do you know that I like orange sari with matching lipstick? Twisting of lips into a charming smile is superb and irresistible.*" Manish wanted say but maintained quiet.

"What are you thinking Manish?" asked Pushpanjali, looking quizzically into his eyes as if trying to read his mind. "How do I look?" she asked after a brief pause with an enigmatic smile.

"Nice choice of dress. You are dressed to the occasion," said Manish, trying to be modest. "You are looking wonderful today."

"Only today?" she asked with wicked grin.

"I mean you are looking wonderful and gorgeous today also."

"Thanks Manish, I feel easy and comfortable in this dress," beamed Pushpanjali alluringly. "I imagined you would also like it.

"Maintain this graceful facial expression during presentation," said Manish. "Should we move now?"

"Yes."

They sauntered along to the car with easy strides. She sat on the driving seat and Manish took the other front seat beside her.

She was driving comfortably in the right lane when suddenly a car jumped out of a nearby parking space right in front of them. She slammed on her brakes suddenly, skidded, and missed the other car by just a few inches. The driver of the other car started yelling at them. She also got angry, but Manish gestured to calm her down. He just beamed and waved at the guy in that car, as if he was really a friend. Stunned, she looked at Manish. She was surprised to notice that he was, as usual, calm, unruffled and composed as if nothing has happened.

Pushpanjali asked annoyingly, "Why did you do that? This guy almost ruined this car? We would have been hurt too."

"Would have been, but not . . . Thanks God we are safe," he explained with composed mind. "Pushpanjali, many people are like garbage trucks. They run around full of garbage and frustration. They spread anger, disappointment and misery where ever they go. They dump them on us. Don't take it personally. Just smile, wave, wish them well, and move on."

"I cannot do that," interrupted Pushpanjali. "I cannot tolerate such activities and irresponsible behavior."

"Calm down dear. You cannot change them, but you can forgive them."

"They deserve to be punished for their irresponsible behavior."

"If you harbor resentment against the offender, who will be hurt? It will be you who suffers," said Manish with soothing voice. "Forgive them darling. Forgiveness is for you, not for others. You will feel happier and more tranquil. Why should you take their garbage and spread it to other people at work, at home, or on the streets. Successful people do not let garbage trucks take over their day. Love the people who treat you right. Forgive the ones who don't," explained Manish placidly. "If you maintain sang-froid during difficult situation, you will get lot of mental piece. You will be enormously benefitted."

"It is difficult for me to control my reaction in such a situation. I will, however, keep your beautiful suggestion in my mind."

"I will tell you how to be in control in such a situation."

"How?" she forced her frozen and dry lips into something resembling a feeble smile. She still had vestiges of fear and exasperation in her mind.

"By taking charge of your emotions and reaction and practicing cooling meditation."

"How?" Pushpanjali repeated the question looking at him briefly and lightheartedly.

"When you are infuriated, sit in a comfortable position, spine erect, feet flat squarely placed on the floor and relax. Observe your breathing for a few seconds. Bring your attention back on breathing when it drifts. Breathe slowly, effortlessly and deeply. Then curl your tongue in shape of a tunnel, as if you are going to sip water through tongue. Create sipping sound. Inhale and feel sensation of cool air in the throat then exhale through nose. It is useful when you are angry and feeling hot. Do not do it now, but keep in mind to practice it when you are free. Remember; never practice it while driving. I repeat, never practice any meditation while driving. Wait for red light or stop the car on side of the road till you calm down."

"Good advice I will practice it and I will let you know the outcome."

"It is our life. We should be responsible for our thoughts, feelings, actions and reactions. Pull your own strings dear," muttered Manish with smile, putting his hand on her shoulder. "Now relax, be present now in this moment and come to the point and discuss about presentation. You have to be in a good mood, my dear sweet Pushpi. You look more beautiful when you smile. Smile is the second best thing you can do with your lips."

"Not 'second best' only 'best'. Do not try to be smart," she said smiling and laughed loudly.

"These are your lips and it is up to you how you use them but use wisely," jested Manish, laughing loudly.

"Enough . . . Now come to the point."

"While on stage, keep 5Ps in mind; Pause, Pitch, Pace, Projection and Pronunciation. Use electronic device whenever possible and check it in advance, if it is working properly."

There was red light, so she stopped the car. "Uff! This is the 5th red light in the row. Do not you feel bad about it? You drive daily on this route," she said annoyingly, with a deep sigh. "We are being delayed."

Manish said, "Again exasperated? Cool down dear. Here also you require re-adjusting your attitude. Probably you did not notice 8 green lights. I noticed and expressed my gratitude to God for so many green lights today."

"Oh, Really? I did not notice."

"Because you were thinking about red lights all the time. What you pay attention on grows. Change your attitude and pay more attention on green lights."

"Still, if I encounter red lights?"

"Utilize the time in a better manner."

"How?"

"As I told you just now, utilize these moments for short-term meditation and relaxation," explained Manish. "If I encounter red light for 1 or 2 minutes, I try to bring my mind into harmony with inner body. I use this time for inner quietude and attaining 'no thought' or 'thoughtless' stage. I use these instances fruitfully for relaxing meditation. You can also utilize this time for cooling meditation about which I just told you. Or you can simply practice deep breathing and relaxation."

"I am astonished how you do that in such a short time?"

"Why short time? If you have red light for two minutes each, 20 times, you will have 40 minutes of mental peace. During this time you can let your body go limp, take in deep breath. You will feel joy, peace and relaxation enter your body on every inhalation and feel stress and anxiety come out with every exhalation."

"Oh great, I will be lucky to get plenty of time to relax on the red lights," quipped Pushpanjali smiling. "What else we can do in traffic jams?"

"There are so many things to do. We can look at each other lovingly and deep into the eyes of each other till the light turns green. If we have to wait longer, we can come out of the car and dance," He said laughingly. "When I am in a jam with a beautiful lady like you . . . wow . . . it is blessing in disguise . . ."

"My dear, I am asking seriously," she mumbled with a broad grin.

"I am serious Pushpanjali. Do whatever you like, but do not allow stressful thoughts to enter your mind," said Manish adroitly changing the topic. "If you are held up in a jam, you can visualize nice day ahead and set intentions of the day. You can do long term and short time planning. If you are lucky enough to get regular traffic jams in your way, you can learn so many things, even a foreign language. You can also listen to motivational audio recordings. The main point is that, you should make the best use of your free time."

"We will not even know when red light turned into green," clucked Pushpanjali laughing.

"Do not worry, there is always a car honking behind you to alert you, when light turns green," he said guffawing. "After relaxation our senses become more alert and responsive."

She stopped the car arriving at the venue of presentation and both got down. There was a big and beautiful lawn and many persons gathered there. All appeared to be in a good mood. Overall ambiance was pleasing. They walked together and reached the big hall where event was to take place.

"Your time starts now; you should talk, walk, shake hands, smile and communicate with full confidence," affirmed Manish. "Today's topic 'Self-esteem' is very nice. It is a wonderful topic. You have already done lot of research on this subject. Do you feel nervous?"

"Slightly, only a few butterflies in the stomach."

"Let them remain there only, dear. Some anxiety is natural and it is help, not hindrance in the presentation. Do not take it as stress, label it as an excitement."

"Okay."

"Imagine you have just earned a million Dollar lottery and you are overwhelmed with euphoria. There is not much difference between stress and excitement. Have, faith and hope that you can do it," murmured Manish reassuringly, putting his hand on her shoulder. "You should be aware and in control of your thoughts and do not allow 'little Pushpanjali' overwhelm 'magnificent and marvelous Pushpanjali'. Do not underestimate yourself. You are better than you think."

"Thanks Manish, I feel greatly motivated. I will keep your suggestions in my mind."

"Do you remember your last best performance, thunderous applause and appreciation you received?"

"Recall, how you behaved, felt and responded. Order the same feeling now," said Manish. "Keep your eyes moving during presentation from person to person; do not stare at anybody or a blank space. People will notice the difference."

"What about movement."

"Feel free to move, but move only when it is necessary. The movement should be limited and purposeful."

"Okay. Thank you very much for your timely advice," said Pushpanjali. "Sometimes I feel that I am being judged when I notice so many eyes on me."

"Remember that audience is your help not hindrance. They want to hear you and see you manifest your best."

"Now come to the conclusion part. Tell me how to conclude."

"Conclude your speech with grand finale and mention again important points in brief, when you conclude. Do it with ease and slow pace and walk with grace," advised Manish. *"Every Great Dream Begins With A Dreamer . . . Always Remember, You Have It Within YOU . . . The Strength, The Patience, The Courage, The Determination And The Passion To Reach For The Stars.!"*

It was a nice and enormous theatre type hall and it was filled with a huge gathering from different colleges of the city.

Two participants were called before Pushpanjali. She minutely observed their performance and waited for her turn with relaxed mind. Pushpanjali's name was announced. She stood up with confidence.

"Wish you best of luck, Pushpanjali. Manifest your best," said Manish smiling. "I know you can do it."

She was the third participant to speak on the subject. She walked confidently to the dais, stood squarely on her legs, shoulder width apart. She smiled, took deep rhythmic breath and waited confidently till all the eyes were on her.

She started, "Good morning ladies and gentlemen. I am Pushpanjali. I am doing my post-graduation from Delhi University and I am representing here Delhi University. Thank you all for giving me an opportunity to share my views with you."

She paused with a relaxed smile. Her confident demeanor amply showed that she was calm and under control. Her gestures and movements were graceful. All eyes were on her when she started after a pause.

"We are all unique creations of God and there is no one like us in this world. I am grateful to God for so many assets and abundance He has given us," she continued with resonating voice with slow pace. "We are great fighters since our conception. We all survived the battle as there were billions of possibilities for the type of children to take birth."

She paused briefly and then continued with grace.

"We are better than we think. We have all wealth and abundance we require. We are in the process of getting all we need . . . We have proclivity to underestimate our capabilities. Recognize your worth and appreciate it and be grateful to God for it. God has given you so many things. You have billions of receptors in your eyes and ears. You have a brain with billions of nerve cells which help you see, smell, hear and detect temperatures. This is the most efficient computer you can ever imagine. You can speak and calm stressed and angry persons. You can cheer unhappy person. You have power to choose. You have power to love."

There was vigorous clapping and all cheered her with gusto. She paused with a smile. Liberated from uncertainty of her own performance, she briefly glanced at Manish also, who was looking at her with appreciation. He nodded approvingly and put the tip of index finger on the tip of thumb to signify his appreciation and indicate his satisfaction at her superb performance.

"If we have self-esteem, we are comfortable within and with ourselves, and this feeling of comfort is very important and has a direct bearing on our performance. If you have a high level of self-esteem, you will be confident, happy, highly motivated and have the right attitude to succeed. Never underestimate your capabilities and always have a high regard for yourself. Know, relish and honor your exceptionality and individuality. Be confident and contented with what you are and you have," she added and continued. "Here I am going to tell you some visualization exercise to instantly gain self-esteem and requisite confidence. You can do this exercise, whenever you like."

She paused and took a few sips of water and continued with mild smile. There was silence and everybody was listening spell bound.

She added energetically, "Never let your self-esteem be tarnished by remnants of failures. Love yourself and you should never feel guilty for loving yourself. So many relationships fail because we have not learnt to love ourselves and accept our uniqueness and rarity. You can possibly not love anyone else unless you love yourself. Heightened self-esteem is a desirable asset and it helps you be a happier individual and face challenges of life with zeal and enthusiasm. Keep yourself safe, fit and happy; only then you will be able to help and make others happy."

Everybody was listening curiously with full attentiveness. She paused and continued speaking in captivating way.

"Suppose you are feeling dull and de-motivated. Imagine a small black and white picture of this 'dull you'. Also imagine bright, colorful and life size picture of 'brilliant and successful you', which reminds you the situation you had won some sports event and you got thunderous applause and you were full of joy and self-esteem. Imagine the picture of 'brighter you' is uttering words, 'I am happy and terrific now in this moment and I am unique creation of God'. These words are constantly echoing all around."

Everybody in the hall was listening with great interest. She took a few deep relaxing breaths with smile dancing on her lips.

She continued, "Imagine that this bright and pleasant image overwhelms the dull picture of you. Also imagine that there are millions of colored zerox of the 'brighter you' picture. You toss all these pictures into the sky. You are listening words, 'I am happy and terrific now in this moment and I am unique creation of God' from all sides, emanating from millions of brighter pictures moving around in the sky. Visualize the terrific feelings you have."

There was thunderous applause. She responded with friendly nod and further added with relaxed smile, "Imagine that you are writing your own auto-biography. You are sitting relaxed and happy in a meditative state. Now, think about the person who loves you very much. He may be your close friend, someone you loved or your mother. Imagine the person enters your body and dictates your auto-biography to you. What you will write in that situation in your auto biography? This is 'you' having self-esteem."

She told to audience some more stories and relevant affirmations. It was a magnificent speech. She recapitulated salient points and came back to her seat as confidently as she had gone to the pedestal. She gracefully left the dais after acknowledging the applause with a smile. Thunderous applause was still echoing in her mind.

When she returned after delivering presentation she was very happy and contented. She hopefully waited for the evaluation to be given by the chief guest. He was all praise for her. He praised her content of the speech and her potent delivery. He said that Pushpanjali had put forth her excellent ideas with confidence, composure and conviction and she maintained throughout her speech, proper pace, pauses, poise and projection. He also praised about delivery of a few more speakers who had also performed well.

He announced name of Pushpanjali and requested her to come to stage to receive the gold medal. She got befitting clapping and loud applause of the huge gathering. Everybody was congratulating her for her excellent delivery.

"The way you started, I knew that you will be the winner in this event. The winning attitude was visibly reflected on your face," squeaked Manish, beaming with bright smile. "You maintained poise and suitable pace. Well done Pushpanjali. I am proud of you."

"Your presence made a lot of difference. Your timely advice was also very helpful," she said with a radiant glow. "You are a constant source of inspiration to me."

"So what next, should we move now?" asked Pushpanjali.

"Yes. You deserve a sumptuous treat. Let us go first to some decent restaurant in the way. We will celebrate your lovely performance and have coffee."

"Let us go to the open air restaurant beside the lake. You will love it. Once I went there with Parinita, my sister. We had wonderful time there."

CHAPTER 4

They reached the place and headed to sitting place under umbrella surrounded by beautiful flowers. Cold wind was blowing and ripples on the lake water were adding to beauty of ambience. White ducks were pedaling silently among colorful pink lotuses. Some ducks strayed into the path of other ducks who were showing their annoyance by flapping their wings. Both watched their activities interestedly. It lasted only for a few minutes. Now the lake was placid and ducks were pedaling along peacefully together without any resentment with each other.

"See, how quickly they forgave each other and moved ahead, as if nothing has happened," said Manish. "They very well understand the importance of forgiveness. It is good for all."

"Yes dear . . . How is this place, Manish?" asked Pushpanjali smiling, adjusting strand hanging on her gorgeous glowing face.

"It is beautiful experience to be here with you. Your attractive smile and sparkle in your eyes makes it even more beautiful. You remind me a poem by Joh Celes; *Smile and get forever praise; . . . Smile man smile! Smile all days!*" said Manish. "May I know, what is secret behind your beautiful smiles? They never fade."

"Smiling is a comforting and pleasing behavior. Everybody feels happy to get it, including you," said Pushpanjali with even a brighter grin. "I always keep in my mind, '*A smile costs nothing, but gives much. . . . Give them one of yours, as none needs a smile so much as he who has no more to give.'"*

"Very suitable quotation," chuckled Manish. "Now I know the secret behind your charming grins."

"Let us stroll around the lake for some time, if you do not mind."

"Sure, I will be glad to amble around with you," said Manish smiling joyfully. They walked together around lake, hand in hand.

"I have a suggestion for you dear Pushpanjali . . . I know you are, nowadays, busy with your preparation for Civil Services Examination and do not have much time at your disposal to spare," said Manish with concern. "This week I am organizing my workshop in Delhi, next week in Bombay and next month in Calcutta. I want you to be trainer for these three workshops. You are a very good speaker and I know that you can adroitly handle these programs after doing some preparation. These workshops will give you opportunities to further sharpen your tools."

"Thank you dear for your concern. You are a great friend and I am proud of you. This week I will be busy with my coaching and studies. I can, however, accompany you to Bombay next week. I want to join it first as a trainee and as an apprentice. I feel that at least some experience is needed to conduct such a workshop. Next month, I am sure, I will adroitly handle it in Calcutta."

"Will your parents allow you to go with me alone? Indian parents, generally, do not give that much freedom to girls."

"I have told them in detail about you. They have confidence in you and me both," she reassured and said smilingly with a measure of certainty. "We have confidence in each other and in ourselves, and that is more important. We are mature adults and we are responsible for our thoughts, feelings, emotions and actions. We have to pull our own strings and live our life, as we desire."

"Great."

"You have tremendous knowledge in the different fields. You might be doing lot of reading in your spare time. Do you write also?"

"Yes I am a voracious reader and I have some fixed hours to study daily. I write also on a regular basis."

"What sort of writing?"

"Books, articles and blogs"

"Have your books been published?"

"Yes, three of them and two more books are on the verge of completion."

"That is marvelous," said Pushpanjali with appreciation. "I am impressed."

"Do you also write?"

"I also write blogs and articles to satisfy myself. I am not getting much time because of my preparation, but plan to write autobiography later."

"Great idea. You have the requisite talent and I am confident that you can do it. I, however, want you to keep one suggestion in mind. Do not underestimate yourself and do not settle for mediocrity," affirmed Manish convincingly. "Manifest your best."

"I think it is time to move. What do you think? Should we move now?" asked Pushpanjali.

"No dear, why are you in hurry?" said Manish reluctantly with a wicked smile. "I have not even looked at you properly."

"Really? What have you been doing so far?" she squeaked joyously. "I am expert in watching a watcher and a thinker. I can easily find out even what you think after watching, darling."

"I like your sense of humor. I had wonderful time with you," said Manish with a charming smile. "Thank you for your pleasant company, I relished every moment. Your presence in my life has made my life beautiful."

"Thanks sweetie. You have given your precious time and did enough to help me," chuckled Pushpanjali wit enticing smile. "I hope you remember Parinita's birthday, day after tomorrow. I want you to be there."

"I will be there," said he reassuringly.

"Do not forget that someone will be eagerly waiting for you," she said smiling and blushing profusely. "Your presence in my life means a lot for me. Please do come."

"I have an urgent and important work to do. I have to supply training material to one of my clients by day after tomorrow, but I am sure, I can manage it in time and I will be there with you all in the evening," said Manish smiling reaching across and putting his hand on her shoulder. His tone was reassuring. "I promise, I will certainly be there in time darling."

"Parinita was very happy to know that we have become close friends. It was a pleasant surprise to her. She discussed a lot about you and Himanshu.

They are class fellows and good friends. They are preparing for engineering entrance exam together. Parinita has invited your brother Himanshu also."

"Yes, I also discussed with Himanshu about you and Parinita. I also know, now, that they are very close friends and doing their studies together most of time. I think they are immensely happy together and they meet often."

CHAPTER 5

He woke up hearing clang of rhythmic bells from a temple nearby, mixed with chirping of birds from adjoining trees in the morning. He got up fresh and was walking in the lawn when he saw his brother Himanshu emerging from his room.

"Good morning brother. How are you? You appear to be fresh and relaxed." said Himanshu jubilantly. "I also got up early as I had to do preparation for engineering entrance examination. There is so much competition nowadays. Lot of hard work is needed to get through."

"It is true. You will definitely make it, as you are so eager to get through this exam. You require such passion for getting success. If you want to get something, you have to infuse enough passion in it. Put your best foot forward, visualize magnificent day ahead and manifest your best," said Manish. "I know you have got the grip of bulldog. Once you decide about something, you get it."

"I am working hard and doing studies according to priorities."

"That is great. You should be ready to work smart and pay the price for fulfilling your passionate desires. Keep your mind on things you want and away from things you do not want."

"Yes brother, you are correct."

"Enthusiasm and passionate desire change mediocrity to excellence. Do not let this fire of passion subside. Water turns into steam with a difference of only one degree in temperature and steam, thus generated, can move some of the biggest engines in the world," said Manish. "With such a devotion, nobody can stop you achieving you cherished goal. You should work not only hard, but smart also."

"What do you mean by working smart? Please explain it in detail?"

"S: Specific. Be specific, for example, complete 15 exercises today. M: Measurable, so that you can monitor progress. A: Achievable, otherwise it will become frightening. R: Realistic; to lose 50 pounds in 30 days is unrealistic, set only realistic goals. T: Time-bound. Adhere to starting and a finishing time," said Manish. "Keep your visions, mission and chief aim in mind and leap ahead to get what you desire. Have faith in your competency and in enormous power of God."

"Great advice, brother. I feel immensely motivated and inspired. Your suggestions are always inspiring and helpful to me. I will work smart with passion to achieve success. Thanks for motivating me. Please give me some more suggestions," requested Himanshu.

"*A young man once asked Socrates the secret to success. Socrates told the young man to meet him near the river the next morning. They met as planned. Socrates asked the young man to walk with him toward the river. When the water got up to their neck, Socrates took the young man by surprise and lowered him into the water. The boy struggled to get out, but Socrates was strong and kept him there until the boy started turning blue. Socrates pulled his head out of the water and the first thing the young man did was to gasp and take a deep breath of air. Socrates asked, 'What did you want the most when you were there inside the water?" The boy replied, "Air." Socrates said, "That is the secret to success. When you want success as passionately as you wanted the air, then you will get it."*

"It is a magnificent story. I will follow your guidance. I will put your suggestions into practice to get best possible results. Let us go to Zonal Park for a walk," said Himanshu. "Weather is also very pleasurable."

"Great idea. Let us go. I also feel like going out."

"I often come here for jogging," said Himanshu.

"You should also exercise and meditate here. This is a lovely place. Exercising in nature is a very good option. By doing this, you will feel energetic for the whole day. I always do meditation and power walk in the natural places like this. I start with breathing exercise, meditation and then do stretching and power walking."

"What is power walk?"

"Power walk is a cross between walking and jogging."

"Can you tell me in detail how to do meditation and power walk?"

"Ok, I tell you . . . You can first sit down cross legged on the ground and relax . . . Choose a quiet place where you will not be disturbed . . . Do not extra effort to breathe, just be aware and breathe normally. Also do not have any expectation for this practice, just be yourself. Do it with effortless ease, as hairs grow and fishes swim. It is spontaneous process."

"Okay."

"Do not try to alter your breathing for a few seconds. Take a relaxed, slow but deep breath. Be aware of your breathing and focus attention on inflow and outflow of breathing. If attention drifts, bring it back gently in the moment. Listen to the air moving into your body and feel your lungs swell. Also observe up and down movement of your belly. Breathe out slowly, but completely through your mouth, letting the air escape on its own. While doing it, be aware of inner body and feel energy in every part of your body."

"Okay."

"Imagine you are inhaling unconditional love, beauty, happiness and peace inside and exhaling disgust, irritation, anger, jealousy out of your body with every outbreath. Continue for some time, till you feel relaxed and rejuvenated," expatiated Manish.

"Does recitation of some 'mantras' or words also help?"

"Yes, when you are relaxed, try to repeat following words in your mind, with a pause between each repetition. Feel each word, as it reaches your consciousness and ripples through your body: serenity, tranquility, peace, love, joy, harmony, gratitude, love, serendipity, melody, mellifluous. You may frame some autosuggestions of your choice to repeat in your mind."

"Thanks for telling me in detail about the breathing and meditation. Now please tell me how to do power walk," requested Himanshu. "What type of accessories are required?"

"For power walk, opt for running shoes rather than walking shoes that flex most at the ball of the foot. Choose shoes that are flat. To start stand up straight, without bowing your back or leaning forward. Holding your core straight will help your muscles work together and increase your walking speed. Look ahead, not down, and focus on a point about 20 feet in front of you. Relax your shoulders. Hold your abdominal muscles firm."

"Where should hands stay?" asked Himanshu curiously.

"Keep your arms and hands close to your body."

"Straight or bent?" asked Himanshu.

"Bend your elbows to approximately 90 degrees. Allow your hands to relax in a slightly curled position. Swing your arms forward, alternating with your step."

"How far?"

"Your hands should not go beyond your chest height while swinging."

"How to move feet?"

"Roll your feet as you walk. Stride forward with one foot, with your heel striking the ground first. Roll your foot forward and push off with your toes. Bring your other foot forward just as you are pushing off with the toes of the front foot."

"Thank you brother for elucidating everything in detail," said Himanshu with joy. He appeared amply satisfied. "I have observed you studying a lot nowadays."

"Yes."

"Are you also preparing for some competition or busy with some project?" asked Himanshu.

"As I told you earlier, I have started organizing motivational training programs in different cities. It has always been my passion to be a life coach and help maximum persons live a life of joy, peace and serenity. I also wanted to have a company of my own and take my company to the pinnacle and make it one of top ten companies in this field."

"Have you made any significant progress? Are you getting sufficient response from people? What are you doing for its promotion?"

"Recently I have organized a few seminars and training programs in the different cities successfully. In recent seminar at Calcutta we have converted 147 persons for 2 day training and 20 persons for a bigger 6 day trainer's training program. 4 persons are coming from UK."

"What is this trainer's training program?"

"I have started the higher level trainer's training program for those who want to establish their own training business."

"Great start," said Himanshu. "I am sure you will create wonderful example for others. This is a respectable profession and it will benefit so many creative persons who want to start their own business and those who want to live an effective and meaningful life. This is a great service to humanity. Your gesture will provide tremendous help to those creative persons who are in search of a job or want to start their own venture."

"Thanks Himanshu," said Manish smiling. "Are you going to Parinita's house on her birthday?"

"Yes, I will be there. I have planned in advance to attend it," said Himanshu with a smile. "May I accompany you to her place or will you reach directly there from your office?"

"I will pick you up and take you with me," said Manish softly, putting soothing and loving hand on his shoulder.

"Thank you very much brother. See you in the evening. I will be ready."

CHAPTER 6

There were around 20 persons in the party. Arrangement was decent. DJ was there and music was creating environment vivacious, effervescent and vibrant. All were chatting joyfully in a comfortable environment. Pushpanjali and Parinita both came to receive Manish and Himanshu and welcomed jubilantly.

"Wish you very happy birthday to you Parinita," said Himanshu and Manish.

Pushpanjali said. "Thank you. Your presence has made this moment even more spectacular. In fact we all were talking about you. Mom and dad were also asking for you. They are there, let us go and meet them first."

"Looking fabulous and sexy sweetheart," whispered Himanshu slowly in the ears of Parinita. "You are irresistible."

"Shut up Himanshu, behave," said Parinita with fake anger.

"Magnificent dress, you are looking charming," said Himanshu looking in the eyes of Parinita with bright grin.

"Thank you Himanshu," she chuckled with amusement. There was no trace of annoyance this time in her voice.

Pradeep and Prachi were already looking at them with affection. They hugged Manish and Himanshu. Both were happy to meet them.

"My both the daughters are talking about both of you all the time," said Prachi, their mother.

"We missed you both," said Pradeep. "I am glad you are both here. You have made this party a great and joyful event."

"You are great mom and dad. You are enthusiastic and energetic and have lot of positive vibrations. You are great inspiration for us," said Himanshu. "Parinita and Pushpanjali have great regard for you and they are proud of you. They are all the time talking about you and your positive mental attitude."

"Thank you Manish, thank you Himanshu," said Pradeep. "We should live, not just exist. I believe in the motto that 'life should be lived fully to question, explore unknown, experience something new, sing and dance, as if nobody is watching, eat, love unconditionally, keep learning new, dare, taste, touch, smell, listen, speak, write, read voraciously, draw, provoke, emote, scream, repent, cry, kneel, pray, bow, rise, stand, look, laugh, cajole, create, confront, confound, walk back, walk forward, circle, hide, and seek, fall down and get up."

"Yes uncle, this is the way one should live. We should live to make our presence felt," said Manish. "We should make best of every moment. Life is too short to be wasted on trifles. Every moment is precious and we should make best of every moment."

"Uncle you are a great inspiration to us. I respect you for what you are and I want to be like you when I grow up," said Himanshu.

"Respect is ok, but you should never imitate others. Be the best of what you are. Everybody is a unique creation of God. Life is changing fast. Keep pace with life. Love unconditionally, live effectively and leap ahead. Live every moment fully with gusto and enthusiasm."

"Thanks uncle."

"Parinita, I think everybody has arrived. Come and cut the cake," said Pradeep smilingly. "Enjoy, as if there is no tomorrow and dance and sing, as if nobody is watching you. Today is the exceptional day of your life and make the best of this beautiful day."

Waves of joy rippled through hall. Everybody seemed to enjoy a lot and everybody was in the state of euphoria. She cut the cake amidst clapping and chanting of 'Happy birthday to you, very happy birthday to you, Parinita.'

Parinita offered cake to everybody present in the party. Music was started and all younger friends gathered together and started dancing. Pushpanjali approached Himanshu and asked, "May I have pleasure of dancing with you, Himanshu?"

"Why not Pushpanjali? It is my pleasure." said Himanshu. "I was, in fact, looking forward to it. Brother told me that you and Parinita are very good dancers and you have trained brother also."

"I think you are correct. We both have learnt steps in a dance school. Now Manish is also good. He has a great capacity for learning new things, whenever possible, from whatever source."

"Especially from this source," he chuckled smiling and looking into her eyes while dancing. "Brother is looking at you surreptitiously."

"Why should he look surreptitiously?" she squeaked. He can look straight into my eyes any time. We are close friends and most of time we are together," she chuckled laughing.

"Now I think you should go to Parinita and dance with her. She is, probably, waiting for you. I will like to dance with Manish now."

"Ok, great, have a wonderful time."

She approached Manish. He was already waiting for her to dance. He readily stood up and started dancing. They were extremely happy to dance together.

"You are a great dancer now. You have improved a lot," said Pushpanjali smiling and looking into his eyes. "Do not hesitate; dance, as if nobody is watching."

"There is no reason not to improve when one gets great teacher like you to teach how to dance," cooed Manish hilariously. "You are an excellent teacher."

"Your sincere efforts have made the difference. You believe in making constant never ending improvements in all fields. You are always eager to learn new things all the time. When you pick up something you complete it."

"Thanks Pushpanjali. Your comments motivate me a lot. When I was learning steps from you, you had advised me to concentrate my energies in the moment and dance as if nobody is watching me. That advice worked wonders."

She said dancing. "But this time your grip is tighter, you are hurting me."

"Oh sorry, should I loosen it a bit? You told me to dance, as if nobody is watching you." He laughed.

"I did not say hug, as if nobody is watching you," she whispered lovingly.

"You are looking gorgeous Pushpanjali. You are irresistible." He whispered.

"Thanks Manish you are also looking very attractive today."

"Really?"

"Yes dear. You are tempting."

"We had great time together. Now it is time to move. We had a great time and enjoyed a lot. Thank you very much for a great party."

CHAPTER 7

Manish got up early. It was a beautiful cold morning. He decided to take a few rounds in his lawn. Wind was blowing slowly, brushing his cheeks. He preferred to practice gratitude walk in his lawn only.

He expressed gratitude to God on every step, walking slowly with effortless ease. He always thanked God for so many amenities he enjoys in his daily life. He also expressed gratitude for the wealth and abundance he had and was in the process of getting. He had perfect faith in God and he believes that God always fulfills prayers of everybody. If He, sometimes does not respond immediately to prayers there may be some valid reason for the same. Time may not be ripe yet or He may have better things in his mind. He only knows what is best for us in the long run. God is always a good God.

He believed that all the prayers are answered but responses may be in different shape. He remembered the prayer: *I asked God for strength, that I might achieve. I was made weak, that I might learn humbly to obey . . . I got nothing I asked for . . . but everything I had hoped for . . . Almost all prayers were answered. I, among all men, am most richly blessed!*

He saw light coming from room of Himanshu. He stepped towards his room. He knocked the door and entered. He was doing some work on the computers.

"Hi brother what is up, I saw you walking in the lawn. How was the sleep?"

"Cannot be better. I had beautiful sleep and got up early, relaxed, in Alfa stge."

"What is Alfa stage, brother?"

"Alfa stage is the deeply relaxed pre-sleep stage in which mind is totally placid and peaceful. You can reach this stage after deep breathing and relaxing meditation. In this stage, mind works with full efficiency. It is the best state of mind to set intentions of the day and visualizing great day ahead," said Manish smiling. "What are you doing now?"

"I am making a list of 100 significant victories of life. It creates winning attitude," said Himanshu.

"Great idea. How do you feel sitting on computer for a long time?"

"Sitting for a long time is problematic. I create a gap and do some exercises, time to time, to relax eyes. I do not sit more than one hour at a time. After some time, I switch over to reading book and other work."

"Very good. I am telling you a beneficial exercise for eyes."

"Oh great."

"Imagine a big infinity sign in front of you. Move your eyes around it for a few seconds after sitting for some time in front of computers, first clockwise then anticlockwise. Palming your eyes is also a useful practice. Rub your hands and softly cup your eyes without touching them."

"Thanks."

"Exercising eyes is not enough; you have to do some more sedentary exercises involving hands, legs, neck and stomach to overcome stiffness. Breathing is very important."

"How should I do breathing?"

"I tell you . . . Sit comfortably on chair or on the flour and observe the breath coming out and going in and relaxing different parts of body."

"Can I lie down?"

"Yes you can, if you feel comfortable that way," said Manish softly. "Simply recline on your back and hands on the sides. Be aware of contacts with the floor. Relax and allow your body to sink into the floor. Continue to be aware of breathing and rise and fall of belly. Feel light and be in a natural free flow mode, like clouds moving in the sky. You may sit cross legged also on the floor, if you feel better that way. Remain quiet for a moment and observe your natural breath with effortless ease. Bring back attention on breathing gently, if attention drifts."

"How deep the breath should be?"

"It should be deep diaphragmatic breath. Feel the diaphragm move downward with a deep inhalation and your tummy expands to accommodate your breath. Take another breath and allow it to escape slowly, being mindful of the movement of your belly with the breath."

"Can you demonstrate?"

"Why not?" said Manish and demonstrated.

"Okay, thanks brother.

"Just keep breathing in relaxed manner, so long as you are comfortable."

"Is it sufficient to relax body and mind?"

"I am coming to that . . . As you inhale, bring awareness to the eyes. Breathe out and let your eyes and surrounding muscles relax . . . Now bring your awareness to mouth as you inhale and relax it as you exhale. Relax lips, tongue, cheeks and nose in similar manner. While inhaling feel the muscles of neck and relax them while exhaling. You can repeat the exercise for all parts of body from head to toe, one by one. Continue for 15 minutes. This way you will be relaxed and tranquil. Take a slow relaxed deep breath and allow your body to feel the sensation of letting go of its tension. Take another deep breath and exhale slowly, again allowing the tension to leave your muscles. Allow it to go, relax completely and don't fight it."

"This is the way to relax. Is there some way to invigorate mind and body further?"

"Yes, to generate extra energy, you have to change your breathing exercise a bit. This style of breathing will overcome sedentary life style tendencies which are associated with heart disease. Sit comfortably on chair, with your back straight and feet flat squarely on the floor. Exhale forcefully, vigorously and completely, contracting your belly," he elaborated in detail. "Passively allow the inhale to come in slowly and easily. Continue doing it for 3 minutes or so, or as long as you feel comfortable. You should reduce the repetitions, if you feel light headed and uncomfortable." He briefly paused here again and demonstrated.

"Great, Thanks brother. Please tell me more about sedentary exercises." requested Himanshu curiously. "Besides deep breathing, what other sedentary exercises are useful?"

"You can, time to time roll your head from side to side backwards and forwards (5) times. Roll your shoulders up and down five (5) times each. Draw a circle with the ankles five (5) times to the right and then five (5) times to the left. Draw a circle with your hands towards the right five (5) times and then five (5) times to the left. Recline on your sofa and slowly draw one knee up to your chest; repeat several times, alternating legs. Stand, raise one foot off the floor and trace letters of the alphabet in the air with one foot; repeat with the other foot."

"I have always found you relaxed and composed. I have never seen you scurrying around or rushing to your work. What is the secret of maintaining pleasant demeanor? What else should in do to develop such an easy life style?"

"I will tell you now about that secret also. I deliberately slow down to the speed of life."

"But by slowing down you will do less and work will pile up."

"No, on the other hand, when you are in hurry, you will make more mistakes, deal with others inefficiently and lose your ability to think sharply, clearly, creatively and intelligently. Therefore, my dear brother, next time you find yourself in a frenzied state, stop and take a planning break. When you have got so many things to do, relax, take deep breath and do nothing for some time. When you start, do it slowly, with less speed. *'Ironically, you need to slow down in order to deal with increased demands.'* said Carlson."

"Great suggestion. Will it make my life happier also?"

"Yes by all means. If you just slow down to the speed of your life, your mundane life will be wonderful. You will live calm composed and joyful life. You know Vikas, the trainer. He once told me, *'I always relish the memory of morning, I woke my wife up. I removed gently hairs from her face and kissed her lovely cheeks. She woke up and smiled. I told her, 'darling there is no hurry, no urgency, you can get up slowly later, after some time. Here is tea I have prepared for you.' She often reminds me that style of waking her up.* We all need to slow down, that's how we are supposed to live. We are all the time running fast and reaching nowhere. Slow down and relish every moment."

"Tell me more, how to do it more efficiently?"

"Just be aware and watch your styles and deliberately slow down. Brain-storm and note down all the things you have to do on a piece of paper or on your Computer. Set the to-do list according to priority. Make weekly and daily planning and set priorities and outline the very next steps you must take over the next few moments. Then, step by step, with a calm pace and focused mind, proceed toward your desired objective."

"Great advice indeed. I will certainly follow your awe-inspiring suggestions."

"You need to keep your mind cool, calm, composed and collected. If you have to switch from one activity to other, do it with an effortless ease. Whatever you do, do with grace ease and lightness and in a free flow mode. Sky is not going to fall and tomorrow is another day. You need to slow your brain down, so you can speed up your performance," said Manish convincingly. "Slowing down is a conscious choice, and not always an easy one, but it leads to a greater appreciation for life and a greater level of happiness. Make the conscious choice to do less. Focus on what's really important. Eat slower, relish every bite. Driving slow is more enjoyable, and much safer. You'll use less fuel too."

"Thanks brother for very valuable advice."

Manish stood up to go, but telephone rang. Himanshu picked up and said, "Good morning dad, how are you and how is the trip. I hope you and mom are enjoying a lot there."

"We are having delightful time here. I have visited so many interesting places. Italy is a very good country. Scenic beauty is also superb. Sometimes we feel nostalgic sick"

"Where is Manish?" asked Sandeep. "We have not talked to him for a long time. We both miss you both a lot."

"He is also here, please talk to him"

"Good morning dad. We miss you a lot. How is the trip to your favorite destination?"

"Good morning Manish. God bless you. We are all fine here, we miss you too," said Sandeep joyfully. "There are so many interesting places to see here. We both are having great time together. I found this place more beautiful than I thought and imagined."

"Be there totally and enjoy every moment. We rarely get opportunity to go out. Make this trip memorable one. See as many places as possible, imbibe the culture and interact a lot. Do not bother about the business. You have properly delegated it and it is running efficiently. We are also visiting, time to time to manage the things."

"Yes, our monitoring mechanism is also working efficiently and we are getting positive feedbacks, time to time, from there. Talk to your mom," said Sandeep joyfully. "Shanti is eager to talk to you and she wants to share lot of things with you."

"Good morning mom, how are you?" asked Manish. "Take care of your health. Are you getting your meals and medicine timely and proper rest?"

"Yes, we are having good time here, but we miss you both."

"We know mom, how much you both care for us. Do not worry. Everything is fine here. We are managing everything efficiently. Enjoy your trip," said Manish reassuringly with soft and loving voice. "You should visit as many places as possible. Do not care for expenditure. Spend on yourself and enjoy every moment being there totally."

CHAPTER 8

Both reached hotel and checked in. It was a five star hotel. 3 rooms were booked, as the trainer, Vikas was also to stay in the same Hotel. Venue of training was also in the same Hotel. They decided to see the venue together with Vikas, who had arrived earlier in the hotel to make arrangements. It was a beautiful conference room with seating capacity of 55 persons. They checked audio and video facilities, which were found to be in perfectly good condition. Manish discussed about the quality of food and other arrangements.

"Thanks Vikas, you have properly arranged the things," said Manish smilingly, putting his loving hand on his shoulder. "You handle prior arrangements and training so precisely that there is nothing left for me to do."

"Thanks Manish," said Vikas. "It is my duty and hobby. I love this work. I feel great to be associated with your prestigious training program. I am inspired by your passion and helpful attitude."

"Vikas, let me introduce, she is Miss Pushpanjali," said Manish with smile. "She is a great buddy and lovely friend."

"I am glad to meet you, Pushpanjali," said Vikas. "Manish is so fond of you. He often talks about you."

"'Thanks Vikas, I heard too much about you and your proficiency and I wanted to attend your workshop."

"You have to groom her to become an adroit trainer for the next training at Calcutta, so that you get ample time to concentrate on trainings in other big cities," said Manish. "See you Vikas in the evening."

"Pushpanjali, let us go out for an outing to nearby park. It is an excellent place and you will enjoy," said Manish turning towards her. "You will feel jubilant and refreshed."

"Okay, great," said Pushpanjali interestedly. "Have you ever been there earlier?"

"Yes, I visited that place earlier with Vikas," said Manish. "It is a splendid place for outing. You will love it."

When they reached there, the park was vibrant with life. So many children were playing there. The breeze was cozy. Children were laughing and running around. Some dogs were barking in the distance. There was sweet aroma of the ripening peaches in an orchard nearby. Young couples were having a picnic under a shady trees, oblivious of others presence. The park was a beautiful and secluded heaven for those willing to relax, enjoy environment and explore the beauty of nature. It had big verdant lawns and a beautiful lake. The privacy and very natural character of each part is what often surprises the visitor. The tranquility and relaxing ambience of the park is what visitors most enjoy.

A restaurant on the park was an excellent place to eat and chat. This natural heaven provided peace and quiet. There was an adventure playground and dedicated areas especially for games and children's activities on the park. They had wonderful time in the park. They walked there for half an hour, took coffee in the restaurant.

"Let us walk towards lake and take boat to go other side of the lake. We will have great time together in the natural surroundings," mumbled Pushpanjali with childlike simplicity. "Have you seen that place earlier? Let us go and see if the grass is greener on the other side of the fence."

"Yes, I visited the other side of the lake once. That is lovely solitary place, more suitable for couples. That day I was alone but today I am lucky to have a lovely company," chuckled Manish smiling joyfully. "Let us go there. I like your suggestion."

It took only 20 minutes to reach the other side of the lake. It was a great experience to travel on the boat in beautiful lake. They heard lovely songs of migratory birds, calling to one another from sky above and from every side. They also heard the voice of the cuckoo emanating from the depths of the wood. Scent of the wood, which follows the rain, was wonderful. The lake was full of lotuses and water lilies interspersed with ducks and migratory birds. They were so thrilled, they jumped out as the boat stopped and started running around with childlike innocence. The bushes were full of fragrant flowers. They enjoyed abundant ambience regardless of showers of drops discharged upon them.

Her feet slipped from a wet rock and she was on the verge of falling when Manish held her with both hands and she hugged him.

"Are you okay? Be careful," said Manish. He felt the hammering of her heart beat.

"Yes, I am okay, thanks Manish," murmured Pushpanjali regaining the composure.

"How did you like the place?" asked Manish.

"It was a wonderful hang out. We relished every moment. Your company made it even more beautiful," she said smilingly. "Let us go back now. It may rain any time. We should reach the other side soon."

"Yes, I agree."

"Let us now take hot coffee in the restaurant, before we go to the hotel."

While returning it started raining. While still under a tree, Manish noticed some cracking sound on the tree. He had premonition of something bad. He stepped back fast and pulled Pushpanjali back with full force. Both fell down and Pushpanjali fell on him. They both saw a branch of tree falling down. But they were both safe. They stood up and thanked God. Had they not stepped back abruptly, the branch would have hurt them. Pushpanjali hugged Manish and thanked him. He could feel the ferocity of hammering of her enhanced heartbeat. He held her in his arms till she regained vestiges of composure.

"Let us sit down for some time," whispered Manish softly raising her chin up. "We will go after 10 minutes. God saved us."

They sat down on a nearby bench and relaxed. Some persons came running for help.

"Are you okay?" queried someone with concern. One lady came and sat with Pushpanjali.

"Yes, God saved us."

Both took rest for 15 minutes. Then moved hand in hand.

"What is happening? Two problems in quick succession," said Pushpanjali.

"We cannot all the time control what happens to us. Sometimes we can control, and sometimes we cannot. But reaction is always in our hand. We should be grateful to God. He is always with us and helps us."

"Do you believe in God?"

"Who does not, do not you also believe?" asked Manish. "Just look around, any time, you will notice his presence. God shaped the universe which is estimated to contain more than 100 billion galaxies. It is only a small manifestation of the inestimable power of God. The collective energy of all the storms, winds, ocean waves, and other forces of nature do not equal even a portion of God's enormous power. Any supremacy that we have is given to us by God. His power is not inhibited by any of His created beings. No task is big for Him. He never fails. He is never tired, frustrated, or discouraged. No problem is too complicated for Him to solve."

"Yes dear you are correct, said Pushpanjali approvingly. "There must be some supreme being who is managing all the things and universe. In Bhagvat Gita Lord Krishna states, *'Know that every being that is glorious, brilliant and powerful is nothing but a manifestation of a small part of my glory.'* He is always there to help and protect us, as we have just seen."

"You are correct. God is all-powerful and He is capable of helping us in many ways, as He has saved our lives. He has the ability and strength to do whatever He pleases," said Manish with gratitude. "And He is never tired, frustrated, or discouraged. No matter what you might be facing, God can help you. Nothing is too hard for Him. No need is too great for Him to meet. No problem is too complicated for Him to solve. No prayer is too difficult for Him to answer. He looks after all of us. We are all safe under his shelter. He never leaves us alone. The light of God surrounds us, the love of God enfolds us, and the power of God protects us and the presence of God watches over us. Wherever we are, God is with us always. No matter in what situation we are, God always with us helps us."

It started raining. Both opened their umbrellas and continued walking. They met an elderly couple without umbrella. They requested the couple to come with them. They gave one umbrella to them and said, "One is sufficient for both of us, we can adjust in one umbrella."

When they reached near hotel, Manish said, "You can take this umbrella with you. I am stopping here. We are staying here in this hotel."

"You are very supportive persons, really very caring, God bless you both. But I cannot keep this umbrella."

"Please take it along. It is still raining. If you do not want to keep it, please pass it on to somebody else who needs it in the way."

"Thank you dear. Did you come here for some business?" queried gentleman.

"I am organizing here, in this hotel, a motivational training program tomorrow."

"Wow great. You are doing a great service to humanity. I was looking forward to such a training program to attend. If you have seats, I will like to attend it with my wife and daughter."

"Yes, you may come tomorrow at 9 in the morning. I will give you special discount. We have special discount for groups."

"Thanks, we will be here tomorrow."

CHAPTER 9

Manish got up early in the morning and got fresh. He did breathing exercise and meditation. He utilized quiet time for setting intentions of the day. He visualized the magnificent day ahead and planned activities to be done during the day. He was happy that Pushpanjali accompanied him to this place. Besides being a great company, she was very helpful in planning and making arrangements for the workshop. Her presence accorded him immense pleasure, therefore he wished to pass maximum time in her company.

He called Pushpanjali on intercom, "What are you doing now? Are you still ensconced in the bed?"

"I am still on the bed floating somewhere between dream and reality. I slept late."

"Why slept late?

"I was thinking about you and so many things which happened during the day."

"Do you want to share?"

"Everything cannot be shared my dear," she chuckled in the pleasant resonating voice.

"I am just going to get up and leave the bed. It will not take me much time to get ready," mumbled Pushpanjali softly, changing the topic. "I will come to your room in 20 minutes. I will have tea and then breakfast together with you."

"Ok darling, I am eagerly waiting for you. We will have tea here in my room and then buffet breakfast in the dining room. You will like it. They have great ambience, aroma and variety."

"Good Morning," she squeaked jubilantly as she entered the room after knocking. She looked fresh and happy. "You are going to have a magnificent day."

"How do you know?" he asked.

You always start your day happily . . . setting intention of the day and visualizing wonderful day ahead," guffawed Pushpanjali.

"There is one more reason, darling, for this day to be beautiful."

"What is that?"

"I am starting this day looking at your gorgeous face and charming smile," squeaked Manish jubilantly. "Let us have tea darling."

"Thanks dear," said Pushpanjali preparing tea. "How much sugar do you take?"

"Half spoon."

"Let us go and walk in the lawn of hotel for some time," said Manish. "Then we will go to the restaurant."

"Okay."

Vikas was also in the restaurant when they reached there. Hall was almost full. There were so many persons enjoying delicious breakfast. Aroma was tickling the taste buds. There were at least 20 types of snacks, fruits, juices, tea, coffee, north and south Indian items.

"Will you like to have omelet? I shall bring it for you also." She brought 2 glasses of butter milk also and gave one to Manish.

"Let us now go to the conference room and see, if everything is properly arranged?" Manish said looking at Vikas and Pushapanjali after breakfast.

Banner was properly displayed at the entrance of the conference room, 'Advance Ahead with Smile' Conference and Lunch.

Arrangement of Coffee and tea was made near the entrance of conference room. Some persons had already arrived and they were enjoying coffee and snacks and chatting with each other. Vikas rechecked the display device and audio system. He found to his satisfaction that the systems were working properly.

All came and ensconced themselves in their seats. Manish introduced himself and Vikas and completed initial formalities. The room was almost full. Natural music of chirping of birds was playing on the audio. Everybody appeared relaxed and happy.

"Good morning friends. I am Manish. I am in training business for pretty long time. Mr. Vikas is here with us. Those who had attended the workshop earlier, know him very well. He has been associated with us for more than two years and he has so far trained thousands of persons in different cities. People were immensely benefitted and a few of them have successfully started their own training programs. Welcome Mr. Vikas. Give him a big hand."

Everybody greeted him with applause. Vikas started speaking, "Thanks Manish. Good Morning everybody. My name is Vikas. I will be your trainer today. Basically I am a doctor and I have been practicing here in this city for 5 years. Attending and participating in different types of seminars and imparting motivational training is my hobby. I have trained more than 5 thousand persons so far in the different cities. I have been associated with Manish for 2 years. He is doing great service to humanity by organizing such activities in the different cities. Life of those who got training has changed a lot. They have learned to live more effectively and joyfully. As Manish has just mentioned, some of them have started their own training program."

He further elaborated, "As you know this is not simply a lecture but an interactive program. Your active participation is very important for getting maximum benefits from this workshop. Please discuss, interact, and put questions relating to your problems of general nature. For specific personal life related problems, however, we will have one to one discussion after workshop. I request you to avoid discussing among yourselves. If you have to discuss anything, please involve me also. I have one more request; switch off your mobiles or put them in a silent mode. If you have to talk on phone, please move out of the room silently."

He further added, "There will be 2 tea breaks and one lunch break. Before I start, I will like to know about you. Where you came from, what are your hobbies, what you expect from this training program and what is your profession?"

"I request everybody to please stand up, move around and get acquainted with each other . . . After doing this, stand in pairs and thoroughly try to know about each other by asking questions so that you can introduce your partner in front of everybody in this workshop." added Vikas after a brief pause.

Everybody chose a partner and did as advised.

"Please sit down and introduce your partner, one by one . . ."

"Please note down on your pad: 5 persons you hate most, 5 blessings you have, 5 top happy experiences in life, 5 persons you love most, 5 dreams you want to achieve in life, 5 worst experiences you had in your life. This basic data will be helpful in our discussions and analysis."

On screen title 'Living in the Moment' appeared.

"Pay attention and be here in the moment. Be aware and bring back your attention gently in the moment when it drifts," said Vikas and paused for the moment till the total attention was drawn to him.

"Here is an interesting story, *'A disciples approached the master and asked, "What is the secret of awakening". The monk took his pen and wrote on the paper, "attention". The disciples said that they did not understand, so the monk again wrote, "Attention, attention, attention". You don't need to try to do or be anything, just be aware and pay attention here and now in this moment. Present moment is the only moment where you can live. Anything else is an illusion."*

Everybody listened attentively with curiosity.

"I assure you friends, you will enjoy here today. This is not simply a lecture but there will be so many practical exercises and games also," said Vikas reassuringly with confidence. "Now, friends, sit down comfortably. Put your feet squarely on the ground, spine erect, back touching backrest of chair softly. Take a relaxed deep breath. Listen to the air moving into your body, and feel your lungs swell. Breathe out slowly but completely through your mouth, letting the air escape on its own. While doing it be aware of inner body and feel energy in every part of your body. Imagine you are inhaling unconditional love, stillness, happiness and peace inside and exhaling disgust, irritation, anger, jealousy out of your body with every breath. Go deep within. Use the inner body as a starting point for going deeper and taking your attention away from where it is usually lodged in the thinking mind. Bring your attention in this moment. Feel energy field inside your body."

He paused and demonstrated.

"Now ask yourself what is going on in your mind. Are you present in the moment, free from past and future?" Vikas said. "Are you relaxed Shams?"

"Yes, now I feel very much relaxed."

"Great."

"Imagine you are a calm deep lake, not surface of the lake. You are sky not the passing clouds. Imagine you are a tree with roots very deeply embedded, stable and placid. Continue breathing; inhale slowly and exhale completely."

Then Vikas further added after a pause, "Affirm slowly as I state, '*My mind is focused on enjoying the present moment. My dwelling place is in the present, however, I visit future, time to time for planning and visualization. I am a tough-minded dynamic optimist and have faith for a brighter future, but I plan for it in the present moment. I sincerely believe that my future will be bright and joyful. I am on the path to a brighter future. Infinite intelligence steers me, guides me and reveals me the plan for unfolding my cherished desire.'"*

Everybody repeated calmly, slowly and in relaxed manner as he instructed.

"Keep your eyes closed. Continue breathing slowly in the relaxed manner," said Vikas. "Here is another equally powerful autosuggestion. Repeat in your mind now, '*I accept my life and everything I have done and I accept my past regrets, knowing they have made me a better person. I am always positive even when remembering my past regrets. I am in the process of rectification of previous wrongs. I have accepted and done the needful about my past regrets and am now ready for the present and future. Accepting and letting go of my regrets is becoming easier and easier and more natural.*' Now open your eyes. How do you feel?"

"I feel great and relaxed," asserted Nina. "Sir, in case I want to solve my problem now, but no solution is in the sight at this moment, as we do not have required facts and data in hand. Problem is creating anxiety and adversely affecting the sleep. What should I do in that situation?"

"Good question. First accept the situation as it is now in this moment. Wait for or arrange the facts focusing in the moment. Till that time, put the problem on the back burner. When you have necessary facts, take decision and start implementing the decision."

"If solution does not exist and there is no possibility of getting it, then what should I do?"

"If there is no possibility of getting solution, accept that too. Note it down in detail on a piece of paper and put it aside to take it up next day with relaxed mind. There is a famous quotation by Mother Goose, *'For every ailment under the sun, There is a remedy, or there is none, If there be one, try to find it; If there be none, never mind it.'"* said Vikas. "I hope Nina you get my point."

"Yes," said Nina smiling. "You have made it amply clear."

"Are past and future totally meaningless?" asked John.

"Past and future are also useful. I mean to say, most of the time make your dwelling place in now. You may visit past for learning important lessons and future for making planning," said Vikas. "Seize the day and make the best of every moment of this day. Always remember this is the first and last day of your life. This is the day, which Lord has made and we should decide to rejoice and be delighted in it."

"I hope all of you are not feeling dull."

"No, it is interesting topic," asserted Reena.

"Still I feel you all require some extra energy. Clapping generates energy. Let us clap," said Vikas and started clapping with energy. Everybody followed laughing and rejoicing. "Do it faster, more vigorously . . ."

"Great, I got lot of energy by clapping. What else should we do remain present in the moment?" asked Reena inquisitively. "Whenever I tried to be in the moment, I found that so many ideas are intruding uninterrupted."

"Just be a watcher, be aware and bring you attention gently back in the moment, if it drifts. Do not worry, if you sometimes fail. With consistent practice you will be more in control. Find work that you like to do and that you find satisfying today, not just the work that may reward you in the future. Love your kids for what they are today, not for what they may become in future. Celebrate personal relationships today, not just at anniversaries and special occasions. Say what you want to say and appreciate now, before it is too late. Kalidas explained, '*Look to this day for it is life, the very life of life. For yesterday is but a dream and tomorrow is only a vision, but today well lived makes every yesterday a dream of happiness and tomorrow a vision of hope. Look well, therefore, to this day such is the salutation of the dawn.*' I hope I have clearly explained the importance of living in now . . ."

He paused and asked, "Anybody wants to ask something?"

Nobody said anything.

"It is time for tea break. Let us go out and have tea and snacks. After this we will discuss vision, mission, passion and chief aim," said Vikas. "We will also discuss how to prepare passion card."

"Please feel free to express your views and ask anything. Always ask, if you have any doubt about the topic we discussed earlier," said Vikas. "Let us go outside and enjoy tea and coffee."

Arrangement for tea and coffee was good. Snacks were hot and tasty.

"Please come inside. You may bring your tea inside if not yet finished."

He paused and waited till everybody came inside and settled on their seats comfortably.

"*A man asked an elderly man, 'Where does this road take me?' The elderly person retorted, 'First tell me where you want to go?' The man replied, 'I don't know.' The elderly person said, 'Then take any road.'* We should never underestimate importance of vision and missions," said Vikas starting the discussion. "We should first decide where we want to go and where we want to reach tomorrow, in a week, in a month, in a year and in five years."

"What is more important long term or short term goal?" asked Prem. "Also please tell me how to find out vision and mission."

"Both type of goals are equally important; one for general direction in which we have to move, and the other for immediate implementation. Big task should be converted into smaller doable chunks," explained Vikas. "*About a hundred years ago, a man looked at the morning newspaper and to his surprise and horror, read his name in the obituary column. The newspapers had reported the death of the wrong person by mistake. His first response was sheer shock. 'Am I here or there?' When he regained his vestiges of composure, his second thought was to find out what people had said about him. The obituary read, 'Dynamite King Dies.' And also 'He was the merchant of death.' This man was the inventor of dynamite and when he read the words 'merchant of death',*" he asked himself a question, '*Is this how I am going to be remembered?' He got in touch with his feelings and decided that this was not the way he wanted to be remembered. From that day on, he started working toward peace. His name was Alfred Nobel and he is remembered today for the great 'Nobel Prize'.*"

"Very interesting," mumbled Mona. "Good lesson, one must know where he is headed. Just as Alfred Nobel got in touch with his feelings and redefined his values, we should step back and do the same . . ."

"This is why we should know our vision, mission and chief aim," said Vikas. "We should know where we have to go."

"How can it be done?" asked Ram interestedly. "Can you be more specific? What actions we should take?"

"You should ask yourself some questions; 'What is your legacy?' . . . 'How would you like to be remembered?' . . . 'Will you be spoken well of?' . . . Where will you like to be after 1 year, 2 years and 5 years from now?' . . . 'Will you be remembered with love and respect?' . . . 'Will you be missed?'"

"Quite relevant questions for self-analysis and finding general direction. Answer to these questions will help us determine where we want to go," said Shams. "What is the next step?"

"We should have long term goals, vision, and mission in life. Create your mission and vision statements. Write down 10 long term aims of life based on your vision and missions of life and also decide the chief aim," elucidated Vikas. "You must write them down and paste at a place where you can refer time to time. Then prepare long term and short term goals and start taking action to implement goals."

"Is there any better way to prepare a list of specific goals to carry as a reminder?" enquired

Reena. "How can we shortlist them after brainstorming?"

"Okay, I will tell you. Everybody, please write down on your pad 10 of your passionate desires you want to fulfill in your life," prodded Vikas. "Now, I tell you how to short list and prepare a passion card to carry with you as a constant reminder."

He paused and waited till the lists were ready.

"When the list is ready, compare 1st desire with remaining 9 in the list, one-by-one. Tick the item which you desire most. Then again take up 2nd and compare with remaining items except already chosen. Thus decide 2nd desire. Now take up third in the list and compare with remaining 7 desires. Continue till you decide 5 top desires. Now note down these 5 desires on your blank passion card attached with your training manual. This is your passion card. Keep it with you and refer to it time to time till your subconscious takes over. Whenever you brainstorm and prepare comprehensive list and prioritize things to do, make sure your list is in conformity with your passion card."

"Now it is time for lunch. We will go to the poolside restaurant for lunch. Let us come back here after an hour. We will discuss anger, resentment and forgiveness," said Vikas.

CHAPTER 10

"I hope everybody is back. So, let us start. Stand up every body and dance," Vikas said smiling and started music.

Everybody was in a jubilant mood. All of them stood up and danced energetically for 5 minutes, till Vikas motioned to stop.

"I hope you all feel dynamic and spirited now," quipped Vikas. "Do you think anger is good or bad emotion?"

"It is a negative emotion like resentment, fear and jealousy," said John. "Obviously it is a bad emotion. So many complications arise in life because of it."

"I do not completely agree with you. All emotions are good and serve useful purpose. These emotions are given to us by God for our self-preservation and survival," affirmed Vikas. "But we have to use them wisely."

"What are the benefits," John asked again.

"Anger is useful for preventing our loved ones doing harmful activity. We can stop people from manipulating us for their advantage with help of anger," explained Vikas. "It is only uncontrolled anger which does the real harm."

"It acts like a hydrogen bomb and if it is not controlled immediately, it does tremendous damage," expounded Vikas.

"Anger is harmful for body and creates problems, then how can I use wisely for our benefits?"

"When you observe resentment arising, control your emotions and be in touch with your thoughts and feelings. With practice you will manage your anger," affirmed Vikas. "You sometimes need anger for restraining people from doing harmful activity and manipulating you. You can still get these benefits just by faking anger, instead of actually getting angry. I hope I am clear. Any doubt Mr. John at this stage."

"No, it is amply clear," said Mona. "How can we effectively control anger?"

"Very good question. Forgiveness is the most effective antidote to anger. I remember a quotation by Catherine Ponder, '*When you hold resentment toward another, you are bound to that person or condition by an emotional link that is stronger than steel. Forgiveness is the only way to dissolve that link and get free.*' When you are angry with someone, you give your controlling in others hand. You punish yourself for others fault. Holding anger is like holding burning coal in your hand to throw it on somebody later on. In such a situation, you are the one who gets burnt," said Vikas. "Whatever the situation, keep your reactions under your control. Explore the cause with a positive mental attitude and take remedial action."

"What more corrective action can be taken?" asked Shams.

"Make your dwelling place in the present moment . . . Forget the past hurt and resentment . . . Develop unconditional love for all . . . Forgive everybody at the earliest opportunity."

"How love helps in controlling anger?" asked Mona.

"When you love someone, you want to see him happy and you wish him be in peace. By doing this you will wish yourself the same thing. You will be filled with gratitude, generosity of spirit and elation," said Vikas. "I am going to tell you how to take corrective action and forgive others, as well as ourselves."

"Ourselves?" asked Mona.

"Yes Mona. Forgiveness is not only for others, it is for you too. When you forgive, you do yourself a big favor, because you get rid of negative feelings bottled up inside you," explained Vikas convincingly. "You are the one who is most beneffitted by forgiving others. You attain more happiness and peace of mind by forgiving your enemies and the persons you hate."

Vikas started very soothing and relaxing music and said softly with smile, "Please be comfortable on your seat and sit erect your back touching softly back of your chair. Put your feet squarely on the ground. Close your eyes and take a deep breath. Inhale slowly for the count of five, hold the breath for the count of three, and exhale completely for the count of five. Continue this way, breathing slowly and completely. Relax and be present in the moment."

He demonstrated by sitting relaxed and inhaling and exhaling. He guided the breathing, counting 1, 2, 3 . . . . and said, "Repeat in your mind, *'My head, my fore head and my eyes are relaxed. My neck and shoulders are relaxed, my chest, abdomen, my heart, my lungs are relaxed. My legs and feet are relaxed. I feel energy in all parts of my body.'* Do as I am doing. Close your eyes and continue till you are totally relaxed."

Everybody did as directed and continued with closed eyes.

"Now think about the person who had hurt you most, and till now you have grudges against whom in your mind. Imagine he is sitting in front of you. Explain to him, how you felt then, how you feel now, and what happened during those hurtful times. After you have affirmed your outlook, let him acknowledge your pain. Watch his reaction and wait for a response. There's a good chance he will understand your point of view."

"Visualize a bright pink light is coming out of you and inundating the person with the light and unconditional love. Imagine that he is becoming happier and more serene. Imagine that resentment against that person is coming out of you as cloud and disappearing in the air and you genuinely forgive that person. You experience feelings of love and serenity within. Now visualize talking with him and saying; *'I forgive you now in this moment forever and release you mentally and spiritually. Now I am free and you are free. I wish you joy, peace, health, unconditional love and happiness. I release you now and all the blessings of life are yours. Peace and harmony reign supreme in our minds. You are both free and feel wonderful."*

"Imagine you hug him and tell that you forgive him. Do this with all of your emotional power and release him from your troubled past."

"You can, later on, at your convenience, repeat the same process for another person you want to forgive. Once you have completed this practice you will instantly feel a great sense of relief," said Vikas. "Let us share our experiences."

"It is a great experience. I feel that heavy burden has been removed from my mind. First I felt lot of agitation within, which later subsided. I feel enormous peace inside now," said John. "I am serene and peaceful within."

"I noticed the agitation on your face and tears coming in your eyes. You appear to be calm, relaxed and still now."

"Yes, I became very emotional. I am happy, I did this exercise. It was a great experience to unburden mind. I wish that I should have done it earlier."

"Shams, do you also want to share some thing with us? I noticed change of your facial expressions"

"First I became annoyed when painful memories associated with that lady were triggered. Then relaxed breathing helped me overcome stressful feelings and I regained placid composure. I was successful in forgiving him completely when I regained strength. I feel very peaceful now and realize that I should have done this earlier. This exercise has totally eradicated my pent up feelings of resentment against that lady. I have also decided to call her and communicate her that I have forgiven her totally and I harbor no grudge against her anymore," explained Shams with a huge sigh of respite. He appeared comfortable and contented. "I also realized today that forgiveness is more for us, than for others. It does more good to us than to anybody else. I have decided today that I will never allow resentment to build up in future. I will immediately forgive, forget and thereby feel peaceful."

"Very good. Thanks for sharing your feelings Mr. Shams," said Vikas with smile. "Prem, do you want to share your experience?"

"I am now serene and joyous, as if heavy load has been removed from my mind. I feel cheerful and stress-free. I never thought earlier that I could ever forgive that person. I totally forgave him and his past behavior."

"Does anybody else want to share anything about the topic under discussion? I hope this is sufficient for today. Let us be here tomorrow at 9AM. We will discuss unconditional love, affirmation and tough-minded dynamic optimism."

CHAPTER 11

"**G**ood morning friends. I hope you all had a comfortable stay and sleep. Two persons are still in the traffic jam and they will be here within 10 minutes. In the mean time we can discuss about yesterday's topics. Does anybody want to ask anything?" asked Vikas.

"I was very peaceful and happy after forgiving the lady who had hurt me. I talked to her on phone yesterday night. I frankly told her how I felt then, in the meantime and yesterday night. She was pleasantly surprised and said sorry for her misbehavior. We are both feeling a great relief and peace," said Shams. "We never imagined that such a change would occur in our attitudes. We felt tremendous reprieve and we are totally free from stress."

"Great," said Vikas, "I remember an expression by Elizabeth Kubler-Ross: *'The ultimate lesson all of us have to learn is unconditional love, which includes not only others but ourselves as well.'*"

"What is unconditional love? How is it different from real love?" asked Peter.

"Both are almost same. The real love or true love is the love in which we love without any reason, without expecting anything in return and in which conditions are not attached. Love is unconditional when you love everyone, yourself and everything without attaching strings and without judging them," expatiated Vikas with a smile. "Love is unconditional, only if it is given freely to everyone, including yourself."

"How to foster such a feeling and develop such a love," asked Mona. "I think, love can survive only when such feelings are there from both sides. Love cannot be one sided."

"You are again putting conditions. Just give for the joy of giving and continue giving without expecting anything in return. You will, in the long run, get more than what you give," affirmed Vikas reassuringly. "Forgive and forget. Have regard and respect for the people you meet. Treat them as equals and not inferior or superior in any way. It requires an abundance of love, especially unconditional love, to heal emotional hurt and restore the beauty and joy in every moment."

"It is not easy to continue loving, if you do not get love in return," said Ram innocently. "Give and take is must, as Mona has said just now, which makes relationship blossom."

"It is not difficult to love unconditionally. This becomes easy, once we take the first step and begin to share our love. You will be amply rewarded by continuous flow of joy, peace and happiness. Real happiness is achieved when you make others happy by constantly giving unconditional love. When we bring unconditional love into our personal, professional, community and family lives, we initiate bringing back joy to our lives. Joy of giving without conditioned attached is the real joy. If you love someone unconditionally, you do not judge, blame or find him bad, said Vikas. "Can anybody give some example of unconditional love?"

"Yes, I tell you a real case. My father had passed away after a long battle with cancer. A friend of mine lived abroad in Canada. He called me to comfort me one day. While on the phone, he asked, 'What would you do, if I fly today and reach your house and give you the biggest hug?' 'I would surely smile with joy,' I replied. Then my doorbell rang and he was standing in front of me. He had reached my place to give me solace in this tragic moment," said John.

"Wow, great," said Vikas. "A few years ago at the Seattle Special Olympics, a few contestants, all physically or mentally disabled, assembled at the starting line for the race. They all started to run the race. One boy faltered and fell down. The remaining contestants heard the boy cry. They all returned back. All of them linked arms and walked across the finish line together. Everyone in the stadium stood, and gave thunderous applause for several minutes . . . Does anybody else want to share some instance?"

"I was an attendant at a local mall. I held the door open for customers and always greeted them with smile. One woman appreciated me for it. She actually told me on several occasions that one day I would make a lovely husband and be successful and happy in life. One evening I walked into that mall after 5 years, holding my wife's hand and the same woman was on her way out. She held the door open for us, winked, smiled and said, "I told you so. If you are helpful, courteous and bless every one you meet, you will always be happy." said Ramesh. "Today I am a successful restaurant owner and she is my Manger."

"Great example," said Vikas.

"I also want to tell you a story," muttered Ram. "A Soldier in a jungle heard painful voice from friend and fellow soldier from behind. He went back to help him against wishes of commanding officer. He came back and informed the officer," He is dead, Sir. "Didn't I tell you he was not going to make it? You could have been killed and I could have lost a great soldier like you. Was it not a mistake to go back?" Harry replied with tears in his eyes, "Officer, it was not a mistake and I did the right thing to go back. I am happy I took the risk. When I reached there, he was still alive and his last words were, "Dear friend, I knew you would certainly come back. In fact I was waiting for you. Now I can die comfortably and peacefully. You fulfilled my last wish. Go back my dearest friend, live your dreams, be happy. God bless you."

"Very touching story indeed," said Vikas. "You cannot live your dream at the expense of others. People who do so are unscrupulous. We need to love unconditionally and make personal sacrifices for our family, friends, and those we care about and who depend on us."

"My colleague told me that twenty years ago he risked his life to save an unknown girl, who was drowning in a river," said John. "He, subsequently, came closer to her and she became his wife. He says he is proud of her. They are extremely happy together."

"I think we have discussed much about various serious subjects. Now there is a need for some change. Everybody please stand up. Choose a partner and stand facing your partner, holding hands of each other, looking straight in the eyes and smiling lovingly," said Vikas smiling. "Decide who is 'A' and who is 'B'. Let All 'A's say to 'B', "*I love you, the way you are, without any condition.*" Let all 'B's say, "*I love you too, the way you are.*"

Everybody did the way they were told.

"A and B, please exchange your roles and repeat the exercise you did just now. Now hug each other for 2 minutes repeating the same sentences continuously," added Vikas. "Close your eyes, feel what you said and heard and accept it . . ."

He paused briefly, observed everybody performing exercise. He studied expressions on everybody's faces and asked, "How you all feel?"

"It was a great feel," Mona chuckled joyfully. "We felt loving and loved."

"I felt appreciated and loved. We should do such exercises often in our daily life," asserted Shams. "Such words with a hug have joyful effect."

"How can we love unconditionally and forgive people in every situation? If we are very soft, the people will walk over us," said John expressing his disapproval. "Sometimes we have to take assertive steps."

"If somebody is trying to take advantage of you, you can assert with confidence and tell the person politely but firmly that you do not like to be treated like that," affirmed Vikas. "Say what you want to say, but do not hold grudge or resentment and love him for what he is."

"Unconditional love works well in relationships too. If you do not put conditions on your spouse and children, you open the doors for a much more fulfilling and trusting relationship," said Vikas. "Unconditional love means love without condition and giving love without expecting anything in return. It is the highest form of love. Without it we suffer from emotional imbalance and disharmony."

"How can we form such new habits?" asked Prem. "Old habits die hard."

"Start doing it now. Take initiative where you are. You might have felt good while doing this exercise. Go out of your comfort zone to help others this moment and put smile on others face whenever possible. Be a go giver. Real happiness is achieved by making others happy," reassured Vikas. "I am going to tell you a great instance told by Mother Teresa, *'One night a man came to our house and told me, 'There is a family with eight children. They have not eaten for 3 days. I took some food and I went with him. When I finally came to the family, I saw the faces of those little children disfigured by hunger. There was no sorrow or sadness in their faces, just the deep anguish of hunger. I gave the rice to the mother. She divided it in two, and went out, carrying half the rice with her. When she came back, I asked her, 'Where did you go?' She gave me this straightforward answer, 'To my neighbors, they are hungry also.' This is a perfect example of 'go giver'. You do not have to be rich to love unconditionally. I am not surprised that she gave because even poor people are and may be generous. She knew that they were hungry. Generally, when we are suffering, we are so focused on ourselves; we have no time for others."*

"Now arrange your seats in a circle. Hold hands of each other, on your both side. Relax and smile. Let your body go limp. Close your eyes," said Vikas and started soft nature sound music. "Imagine your loved ones, your saints, your parents and your soul mates are arriving slowly here inundated in blue light. They are touching you with love and blessing you. They are motivating you to live a joyful life, full of unconditional love. They all combine to become sphere of blue light which enters your body and expands to overwhelm you completely. It goes on expanding to fill the room, the surrounding, the city and the entire universe. There is unconditional love all around. Continue relaxed breathing and be with yourself."

"Now come out slowly, open your eyes sit alert. Clap enthusiastically. You will generate lot of energy. Feel enthusiastic as we are going to discuss 'enthusiasm'," said Vikas. "I hope you are wide awake and relaxed. Now clap vigorously."

He demonstrated with vigorous clapping and said, "Clap faster and enthusiastically. You can be enthusiastic any time. Enthusiasm depends on your thoughts, emotions, feelings and actions which are always in your control. Do you all feel enthusiastic now?"

Everybody was in a jubilant mood and waves of enthusiasm rippled around. Feeling of exuberance permeated the room.

"Yes we feel great and energetic," said Ram.

"Imagine the situation, when we do not feel enthusiastic in spite of our best efforts?" asked

Shams. "Can we still change our attitude and feel enthusiastic and energetic?"

"Can you recall a situation, when you were ecstatic and enthusiastic last time? It may be some social event, sports event or academic achievement."

"Yes, it was last year when I won Regional Badminton Championship," said Shams joyfully. "I still vicariously enjoy that time. Its memory motivates me often."

"Shams, close your eyes, sit relaxed and breathe deeply and completely. Recall the environment and the situation when you won the match. Recall vividly what you thought and felt that time. How people applauded and congratulated you? What did you exactly feel at that time? Order the same feeling now . . . How do you feel now?"

"I feel happy, I feel terrific, full of enthusiasm and elation," chuckled Shams smiling profusely.

"Great, you can infuse same feeling later in any task you have to perform in future," said Vikas persuasively. "You can order this feeling whenever you are feeling dull. Order that feeling when you require."

"Yes, I feel it will certainly be effective . . ." affirmed Shams. "Even then, anyhow, if I do not feel enthusiastic?"

"Then sorry, I cannot help you, only God can," chuckled Vikas. Everybody laughed joyously. "Do you know meaning of enthusiasm? Originally, an enthusiast was a person possessed by a God. Enthusiasm originally meant inspiration or possession by a divine afflatus or by the presence of God. Sit at a quiet place and relax. Then have one-to-one conversation with God. May be, Shams, even then you may not feel enthusiastic."

Everybody laughed.

"There is still one more option to reach cloud nine. If you are not enthusiastic in spite of your best efforts, then fake it."

"But mind will not believe it," said Shams laughing.

"Obviously, mind will not believe it, as it is fake. First you may feel uneasy, but if you continue doing it, your mind will start treating your feeling as real and you will be enthusiastic in real sense. Fake it, until you make it," said Vikas smiling. "Henry Truman said, '*I studied the lives of great men and famous women, and I found that the men and women who got to the top were those who did the jobs they had in hand, with everything they had of energy and enthusiasm.'* Keep yourself excited all the time."

"Is excitement same as enthusiasm?" asked Mona. "How these are related with each other?"

"Enthusiasm is higher stage of uninterrupted excitement. Excitement is something that comes and goes. Enthusiasm, on the other hand, is excitement elevated to such a high level that it sticks with you. It is an outward manifestation of an inner composure, an energy generator and an obstacle blaster. It is also greatest source of competence, supremacy and attainment."

"Enthusiasm generated in winning a game is temporary. How can we have lasting enthusiasm?" asked John curiously. "One may feel dull again when initial euphoria subsides."

"You are correct and I agree with you. Excitement during a championship is temporary. But, as I have told you earlier, you can order the same feeling again and again," expatiated Vikas. "You will generate and sustain uninterrupted excitement and enthusiasm by keeping constantly those euphoric moments in mind. Allow only enthusiastic feelings to enter and remain in your consciousness until conscious mind takes over."

"Tell me more ways to generate and sustain enthusiasm," requested John.

"Sustained and genuine enthusiasm comes through the discovery of your real purpose and vision. Discover your vision and mission. Once you find your purpose, get busy attaining your goals," said Vikas. "Genuine enthusiasm creates energy and dispels panic, procrastination and inactivity. It is a constant source of fabulous achievements."

"I agree. It is a great suggestion," said Neeta. "Enthusiasm contributes a lot for achieving success and happiness. It creates euphoria and overcomes dullness."

"Try to be enthusiastic and happy. Act enthusiastic and be enthusiastic now in this moment. You have a great feeling when you are totally engrossed in an activity which you enjoy doing and which is in conformity with your cherished desire. That time you will be in a flow. You will spend more time in the flow. So next time you find yourself in that wonderful state of flow, take some time to analyze why it's happening and how you can order that feeling in other situations of your life," said

Vikas convincingly. "More success will give you more enthusiasm and you will be in a flow."

"Age weakens our body and dulls our mind. In that situation how can we have such an enthusiasm you are talking about?" asked Prem. "Every system in our body becomes less efficient."

"You are as old as you think and feel you are. Age wrinkles body, not soul. Have you not met some persons who are old, but they are full of energy and enthusiasm?"

"Yes, we have met so many persons in our daily lives," said Prem. "They are more active than so many young persons."

"I recently met a 78 year old woman who was arranging her passport, so that she could go on world tour next month to celebrate her birthday," said Vikas. "There are so many persons who reached pinnacle of glory when they attained age of 80 years or more. Advancing age does not restrain them from getting their esteemed desires."

"How can I develop such a feeling and retain it."

"Find time to sit down, explore, brainstorm and construct a list of things that make you happy and enthusiastic. Put the list where you can see it every day. It will remind you the steps you have to take to make you happy," said Vikas. "Prepare a passion card for your desired goals and values and live your life accordingly. Take first thing first and do work according to priority."

"I also remember an instance," said Pushpanjali. "I was going to Calcutta by road with my friends. I was stuck in traffic jam due to road repair. An aged couple started music on their car stereo, came out of the car in front of us and danced there straight for half an hour. Everybody in the traffic started cheering them and many persons joined and started dancing with them."

"Great example Pushpanjali. Enthusiasm is infectious," said Vikas beaming. "Enthusiasm and success go hand in hand, but enthusiasm comes generally first. Enthusiasm is precious. It inspires confidence, raises morale, and builds loyalty. You can feel enthusiasm by the way a person talks, walks or shakes hands."

"Enthusiasm is a habit that one can acquire and practice," said Manish. "Many decades ago, Charles Schwab, who was earning a salary of a million dollars a year, was asked, 'if he was being paid such a high salary because of his exceptional ability to produce steel. Charles Schwab replied, '*I consider my ability to arouse enthusiasm among the men the greatest asset I possess, and the way to develop the best that is in a man is by appreciation and encouragement.*'"

"Thanks Manish. Now is the time for tea break. After that we will discuss 'affirmation and auto-suggestion'," said Vikas.

CHAPTER 12

After tea break everybody appeared relaxed. Vikas started discussion after everybody arrived in the hall.

"First I will like to know, if anybody wants to ask anything about earlier topic," said Vikas. "Be frank and discuss anything you like."

Nobody buzzed.

"Affirmations are very important in life, as they help us remain on the track and live an effective life. They help us break through negativity and remain positive," said Vikas. "If you repeat them regularly every day, you will notice noteworthy changes in the way you reflect and feel. You will be joyful, serene and focused. Positive affirmations will help you live a meaningful and wonderful life. You can create your own affirmations to suit your requirement and ideology."

"While framing affirmations, what should we keep in our mind?" asked John.

"Affirmations should be short, specific and clear. Affirmations should be for yourself, because you cannot make affirmations for others. These should be in the present tense," said Vikas. "Can anybody give examples of such affirmations?"

"I am happy and relaxed," said John.

"I am always successful," said Shams. "I always live with grace, ease and lightness."

"I plan to lose weight," said Reena.

"Can you be more specific?" interrupted Vikas. "It will be better if you specify exact weight and date."

"I will reduce my weight to 50 kilograms before 1st of December this year."

"That is far better," said Vikas.

"I am in the process of losing 5 Kgs," said Ram.

"I am in the process of having more money and I attract wealth and abundance," said Nina.

"You may combine a few short specific affirmations into complex single motivational paragraph like, "I am happy now and today is the best day of my life. This day will bring me profound peace, prosperity and happiness. Day-by-day, in every way, through the grace of God, I and my family members are getting better and better, more confident and healthier. With help of God, I and my family members are free from disease, infirmities and problems. I have many blessings and amenities, which I could have less and many persons already have less than I have. I am free from problems, which many persons have."

"Can you tell me some more interesting way to effectively practice affirmation?" asked Ram curiously.

"Yes there is. I tell you. Sit relaxed and take a few deep breaths inhaling slowly and exhaling completely. Let the ideas enter your mind freely, with effortless ease. Do not bother, even if a negative idea enters your mind. Just be aware. Write it down on a piece of paper. Also write down opposite of this idea," elaborated Vikas. "Imagine you are playing the negative idea on a tape recorder and its volume control is in your hand. Repeat the idea i.e. "I am sad". Move your fingers, as if decreasing the volume and say the idea a bit less loudly. Go on decreasing volume until it becomes a whisper. Now, softly say, "I am happy." Go on increasing the volume and saying the affirmation again and again. If you repeat it continuously your subconscious will take over."

"This is very effective way to practice affirmation. This process will certainly be effective," said Ram. "Suggest some more exercise."

"Okay, I will tell you a very useful and effective exercise. You will see how effective are affirmation in our lives. To start with, let us form groups of 5 persons each."

He helped in formation of groups. Everybody followed his instructions and moved to form the groups according to their choices. Some gathered randomly.

"Now, attention here and now. Listen carefully. Turn-by-turn one person will sit in the middle and remaining other 4 persons will surround him. The person in the middle will give 3 choicest affirmations to one person and remaining 3 persons around the person will bombard the following affirmations, touching softly and lovingly body of the person sitting in the middle."

"Which are the affirmations for bombardment?" asked Mona interestedly.

"Here is the list for everybody."

1   . . . 'name of the person in the middle' . . . you are loved.
2   . . . 'name of the person in the middle' . . . you are loveable.

3   . . . 'name of the person in the middle' . . . you can do anything you like.

4   . . . 'name of the person in the middle' . . . you are unique and beautiful creation of God.

Pushpanjali and Manish were in the same group of 5. Everybody was to sit in the middle for 5 minutes, till the ring tone was sounded by Vikas. The exercise was very interesting. After 5 minute person sitting in the middle was changed and replaced with one of persons surrounding. Whole exercise took around 25 minutes.

"Anybody wants to share?" queried Vikas. "I have seen tears from eyes of so many persons."

"I had never experienced such an ecstatic feeling earlier in my life. I was on cloud nine. I will probably never forget this," said Ram with serene mind. "I was in the 7th heaven. I felt so much appreciated. I wish I should have done this exercise many time earlier also."

"I was full of self-esteem and euphoria. I never felt in my life so much adored and loved. It was one of the best moments of my life. It was feeling of bliss and elation," asserted John. "I, now, know what it feels to be loved. I was so emotional, I started weeping. These were tears emanated from inner bliss."

"I experienced extreme joy and euphoria. I was feeling very light and serene. I was floating in the heaven like cloud in the sky. Butter-soft touches and euphonic affirmations created magic," said Shyam. "I never felt that much appreciated, earlier in my life."

"Now let us go out and enjoy tea and coffee."

Everybody was happy with this exercise. Pushpanjali came to Manish with a cup of coffee.

"Here are a few more words darling, I wanted to say, but could not gather courage to say in front of others, while doing the previous exercise. I will like to say these to you now, if you do not mind," jested Manish with a mischievous smile.

"Why not," chuckled Pushpanjali suspiciously, beaming with a fascinating smile. She could sense him hesitating, looking sideways and amassing all his powers to speak.

"You are sweet, cute, gorgeous, captivating, stunning and irresistible." He whispered in her ears with a butter-soft voice.

She blushed and looked slightly taken a back, and then she overcame her brief impulse and burst into laughing. She was pleasantly surprised to hear such unexpected words from him. She felt that she was happy to hear these sugary words. Suddenly, feeling self-conscious, she struggled to maintain her equilibrium. Everybody looked at them hearing loud laughter.

"Are you crazy? Everybody is looking at us," said Pushpanjali with stern glances.

"I only whispered in your ears. It was you who laughed loudly."

"Sorry, mistake was mine."

"Is it a private joke or we can also come and join?" asked Vikas laughing, standing away in a group.

"Nothing important Vikas, a simple banter," quipped Pushpanjali, smiling brightly.

"But, my dear Manish, it was not in the affirmation list provided," she remarked whispering in butter-soft and merely audible voice, looking into his eyes with enticing smiling. "Rectify your dangerous affirmation list."

"Do not you like this?" Manish chuckled with wicked looks in his eyes.

"I do not know." She blushed and looked sideways.

Everybody came back in the room.

"Welcome back, everybody," said Vikas. "You can now clear your doubts. Feel free to ask anything you like. Later on, some other days also, you all can be in touch and discuss anything. You will all have our contact nos. Certificates for completion of the workshop will be given at 6PM today."

The camera man had arrived and started taking snaps. Everybody was in a jubilant mood. Certain books and CDs were also displayed in the conference room.

"There is no need to purchase books and CDs, as you all will get the complete set, free, along with training material. You can, however, purchase, if you still want some extra copies."

"Your feedback is very important for us. Please let me know your views in brief on video camera. It will be helpful for us to further improve this workshop. We are organizing such workshops in different cities. You can attend it again next month alone, with friends or with your family members. There is a special concession for those who repeat the course or who attend in a group. We also organize 'trainers training' program," said Vikas.

"This 'Trainers training' program is designed for those who want to start their own training business. The details and training material is given on the pen-drive, we are providing now to everybody," said Manish. "You can call me or Vikas any time for other supports, if you want to organize your own training courses. We will help you with training material, venue arrangement and guidance."

CHAPTER 13

Manish was feeling like having an outing with Pushpanjali. It has been about a week since he met her last during Bombay visit. He could not talk to her on telephone also. He was busy these days disposing off long pending work. Another reason was he did not want to distract her from her studies.

He telephoned and asked her, "What are you doing today dear Pushpi. Can we meet today evening in the lake resort?"

"Why not, I am also eager to meet you," said Pushpanjali joyfully. "I miss you a lot. I was also thinking to call you today. I am glad you called. I will reach there at 7.00 and we will have dinner together."

They both reached there and settled in the corner seat and ordered for soup. Ambience was pleasing. Wall to wall carpet with a big dragon and paper lamps with dim luminance looked beautiful.

"Wow! You are looking great in jeans and white shirt."

"I rarely put it on, but today I did, hoping you may like it."

"You care so much about my choice. Thank you very much. You look even more gorgeous today," chuckled Manish smiling and looking deep into her eyes. "You look so beautiful, I find it difficult to lower the glances."

"Thanks sweetie," said Pushpanjali smiling. "Your comments make me feel special."

"You are marvelous creation of God."

"You have seen the menu. What will you like to have? This place is good for Chinese food. Preparation is superb," said she with amusement. Her eye sparkled with joy. Her smiling face added to her immense charm.

"I will prefer to let you decide and place order. How can I forego your expertise?" said Manish, looking at her with a charming smile. "I always relish your choice. You know more about my taste than I do."

"Thank."

She placed the order, as if looking at the menu, but contemplating and ordering from her memory.

"It is always a joyful experience to share some moments with you," clucked Manish. "I missed you a lot."

"I also feel the same and I also miss you," said she smiling charmingly and looking into his eyes.

"Why you miss me Pushpi dear."

"Do you not miss me?" asked Pushpanjali with alluring smile. "It feels wonderful to be with you, talk to you and look at you."

"I miss you often, but I do not want to disturb you. You are now a days very much engrossed in your studies. It is not easy qualifying the Civil Service exam. There is a lot of competition nowadays."

"Please keep calling me whenever you have time. Your calls are helps not hindrances. You are a constant source of inspiration to me."

"Thanks."

"Look at the corner cabin," suggested Pushpanjali.

"Why, what is there?" asked Manish.

"Himanshu and Parinita are sitting in the cabin. They have probably not seen us yet."

"It is great to see them together here. They appear to be really very close friends. They might be going for outing often. Should we call them here?" asked Manish. "It is a great opportunity for us all to interact."

"Okay. Let them sit together for some time. May be, they require some privacy. Let them have more time together. I have seen them together often. We may call them here after half an hour. I think we also require privacy, don't we?" mumbled Pushpanjali smiling and looking into his eyes. "Let us also have some great time together darling. We are meeting after a long gap."

"Why not dear?" said Manish smiling. "We also deserve some good time together."

She was very happy today and she was enjoying every moment with Manish. She was feeling that she was coming closer to Manish, day by day. She was proud of his friendship.

After half an hour Pushpanjali went to them and said, "Hi Himanshu, hi Parinita. I am glad to see you both here. Manish is also here. Come with me and let us take dinner together."

Both were surprised. Stunned, they looked at each other, as if something unusual happened. Both were struggling to maintain poise and soon regained vestiges of composure.

"It is a pleasant surprise to see you here. Let us sit together," squeaked Himanshu gleefully. Both accompanied Pushpanjali.

"Hi Parinita, Hi Himanshu, I am glad to see you both here. How are you? It is a great opportunity to be here together," said Manish jubilantly. "Welcome you both."

"I am really thrilled to see you both here. In fact, we were planning and looking forward to invite you both for dinner in some restaurant. We actually wanted to discuss with you both, an important matter. Today we are very happy that we got an opportunity to discuss that issue," said Himanshu joyfully.

"Okay, then it is great we met here today," said Pushpanjali."

"You will be glad to know that we both have been selected for admission in the same engineering college. I got electronics and Himanshu got computers. This is exactly what we wanted. We decided to visit this place to celebrate it together," said Himanshu joyfully. "Our happiness is multiplied seeing you both here."

"Congratulations, both of you," murmured Manish. "You both deserved it. Sincere efforts are never wasted."

"I am happy you got your cherished goals. You worked hard and made sincere efforts, studying day and night," said Pushpanjali. "You are both on the right track and you will soon become engineers. I congratulate you both."

"One more thing I want to discuss with you both," said Himanshu hesitatingly and looked sideways at Parinita.

"Tell us, there is no need to hesitate. We are all friends. Your body language has already revealed a lot. I could sense it," remarked Pushpanjali seriously with concerned looks. You are both mature and responsible persons. You were given full freedom to meet and study together. Now do not tell us, 'We love each other so much that we want to marry and we cannot live without each other.'"

"Thanks sister. We were gathering courage and fumbling for suitable words to express our feelings. This is exactly what we wanted to say. You put words in my mouth," said Parinita with a mild smile, hesitatingly with a sigh of relief.

"Congratulations. You will be a wonderful couple. You are made for each other. I am happy," chuckled Manish, his eyes sparkling with sheer joy. Pushpanjali also smiled merrily. Everyone giggled together with delight.

"I am very happy," said Pushpanjali smiling profusely. "I hope our parents will also agree. We will help you convince them. When it all started, by the way? Was it love at first sight?"

"I liked her since the day I met, maybe she also. Only she can tell. We have been close friends for a long time, but I do not remember as to when did we leap ahead into love. Now we love each other," affirmed Himanshu convincingly. "We are both very happy together."

"Let us meet tomorrow for lunch at our residence. We can discuss with parents," mumbled Parinita animatedly. "You both have given me so much courage."

"Okay done," said Manish unequivocally. "I offer to initiate the dialogue."

"Excuse me," Pushpanjali called the waiter. "Please note down some more dishes."

"Parinita, what will you like to have? Pushpanjali has already placed order. You both tell your choice," said Manish. "We should celebrate the occasion."

"We will also take according to your choice today. Add whatever you like," murmured Parinita with soft voice smiling. Himanshu also nodded approval.

"Do not forget to order sweets," quipped Manish smiling at Pushpanjali. "This is a great occasion to celebrate."

CHAPTER 14

They all gathered at the residence of Pushpanjali. All were happy, but Parinita appeared a bit tense. She was staring towards gate expressionlessly, as if her soul was sucked out of her.

"Are you okay Parinita? Cannot you take it easy? You are not alone, we are all with you," assured Pushpanjali with butter-soft loving tone, putting her hand on her shoulder. "Be a tough-minded optimist. Neither worry, nor presuppose any problem. I am sure, everything will turn out to be the best. We will talk to Mom and Dad and convince them."

"I am a bit nervous." mumbled Parinita grimly. She slowly inched towards Himanshu with slow pace. She felt her gaze move to him, her expressions almost uncomprehending. She looked at his calm face and asked, "Cannot we postpone the discussion for some other time in the future?"

"Do not be silly. What has to be done should be done without delay," Himanshu retorted, reassuring her with conviction. "We will discuss today, here and now."

"I agree with Himanshu. You have to act and live in the present. Do not presuppose any problem. You cannot live where you have been. You cannot live where you want to be in the future. You can live only now in the present moment," said Manish reassuringly. "I am sure, everything will be turn out to be okay."

They sat on sofa. Pradeep and Prachi came in the hall and hugged Manish and Himanshu. Everybody greeted them.

"How are you Manish? I have not seen you for a long time. Have you been busy these days?" asked Pradeep with smile. "Pushpanjali has become your fan. She talks all the time about you."

"Yes uncle. I have been pretty busy. There was so much work pending."

"You should delegate some of your work. If you have so much work to do and you have less time at your disposal, you must delegate your work to suitable persons. It is an important and effective time management tool. It may, however, create more problems, if it is not proper and efficient."

"Uncle, how can it be done efficiently?"

"Okay I tell you. First, you find a person who is suitable for the work you want to delegate. Make sure you choose the right person for the job. Never delegate something to someone, unless you are sure that he will be able to handle it, otherwise you will constantly worry about the task instead of focusing on other important tasks. Then you should clarify project description and exactly what is to be done, how to be done and when to be completed."

"Sometime others cannot handle work as efficiently as we can do," said Manish. "They will not understand work properly."

"I do not believe that. Find suitable person and explant to him properly. Ask the person to repeat back to you what you have just described to ensure that he has understood the same," said Pradeep. "There should be good communication. Also, there should be efficient feedback mechanism, assessment, monitoring and measuring system. There should also be arrangement to monitor accomplishment of the task."

"Okay. Monitoring is important."

"Efficient delegation means that you can forget about the task after delegating it, knowing that the person will do the task according to your specifications and in the time-frame you have set. This allows you to focus on other tasks for more efficient time management."

"Good suggestion uncle. Thank you very much," said Manish. "That way I will have ample time for supervision and monitoring. I will find soon a suitable hand to whom I can delegate some work."

"It is great to see all of you together here today. I hope everything is okay."

Himanshu and Parinita looked at each other, their expressions displaying mixture of emotions. Both held breath and waited. Everybody was silent for a while.

"Uncle and aunty I wanted to discuss with you something very important . . ." said Manish. "Himanshu and Parinita are in love with each other and they want your approval and blessings."

"What! Such an important decision and nobody told me earlier," said Pradeep vociferously. He appeared to be taken aback. His face appeared to change colors and expressions. His mellow mood appeared to shift gears to overdrive, "I always knew that they are very good friends and they passed their ample time together in preparation. I was extremely happy to know that they have cleared the examination. But I never thought that your friendship will leap that ahead that too without taking us in confidence."

Pradeep went out of the room along with Prachi. All were looking at each other stunned with changed scenario. They never expected such a situation. Everybody appeared confused.

"This is why I wanted to postpone it," murmured Parinita meekly.

"Be bold, face it with confidence," said Pushpanjali calmly and reassuringly. "Hope for the best and be a tough-minded dynamic optimist."

"Do not worry. I am sure we will convince our parents. You know I am great counselor and life coach," said Manish calmly and categorically. "I am a tough minded dynamic optimist also. I hope consistently for the best. If, anyhow, the desired outcome is still not coming forth, I will make my best efforts to successfully convince them. If I initiate a task, I accomplish it."

Pradeep returned in the hall again. His face was surprisingly calm this time, but expressionless and said looking in the direction of Parinita and Himanshu, "I always believed in your maturity and your wise decisions and allowed you full freedom to study together," said Pradeep placidly. Both stood tense and looking down. They were ready for impending outburst and disaster. Various filmy dialogues were reverberating in their minds.

"I am proud of you both for the best decision you have taken," chuckled Pradeep laughing loudly. "God bless you. I love you both."

He hugged both and asked everybody to come and all hugged together. Prachi was also happy. The suspense had a dramatic end. She came with sweets and offered to everybody. Everybody appeared ecstatic. Parinita and Himanshu were on the seventh heaven.

"It is your life. You are responsible for your thoughts, feelings emotions and actions. I do not want to force my opinion on you, but I want to suggest something. Listen to me first, then you take your own decision, as major decisions about your lives should be taken by you. I always gave you freedom of decision about your life," said Pradeep with butter-soft voice and relaxed smile. "I only want that your studies should not be adversely affected. The marriage should take place when your studies are complete."

"Yes, I agree with you," squeaked Himanshu with jubilation. "Thank you uncle."

"I agree with you dad," said Pushpanjali joyfully. "You are the best person to decide about timings."

"Good advice dad. We also have the same opinion," said Parinita.

"You will be glad to know that I had already sensed this occurrence and accordingly I had discussed this with your parents. They also tentatively agreed and you will not have to convince them," said Pradeep amused, looking at Manish and Himanshu with smile. "We had been acquainted with them for a long time. We have been more in touch recently since you all became friends. Our friendship bonds are strengthening day by day. Day by day, in every way through the grace of God we are all coming closer and closer."

Let us now take lunch," said Prachi with refreshing simplicity, sitting on a dining chair. They enjoyed lunch together. "God bless you and give you all abundance in life."

CHAPTER 15

Pushpanjali was sitting in her study room after having a nap in the afternoon. She was feeling relaxed and happy. She relished the memory of beautiful moments passed with Manish. She heard Parinita and Himanshu talking with each other in soft voice. They were sitting in the adjoining veranda oblivious of her presence.

"Are you coming in the evening for studies?" asked Parinita, her glance still fixed in her book. "I will like to cover some topics jointly with you, especially computers and vocabulary."

"Yes, I will be here at 7.00 in the evening," affirmed Himanshu raising his glance at her. "Do not forget to put on the pink sari I like."

"Are you coming here for studies or for dating," she chuckled joyfully and laughed with muffled voice. "We have to be more serious in our studies. You know dear how difficult it is now a days to clear the exams. Your presence helps me a lot in cracking difficult problems."

"I also feel very happy when you are with me. It is win-win for both of us," cooed Himanshu. "Sometimes, though, it is difficult to study jointly."

"I am sorry . . . Do I disturb you?"

"It is not your fault . . . It is me, who is to blame . . . I have to concentrate on studies at the same time I have to restrain myself from looking at you," Himanshu jested smiling and looking into her eyes. "Sometimes you are irresistible."

"We have, not only to love, but to leap ahead also my dear friend. Concentrate on your studies," she said laughing and hugged him. "I hope this satisfies your craving."

"Thank you darling," said Himanshu hugging her tight. "But some time I think about your lovely lips and vicariously . . ."

"Shut up Himanshu," she retorted blushing profusely. "Do not be crazy. Do not forget our deal to be just friends, not couples, till the time comes."

"Okay darling."

"Let us complete the remaining assignments," she said with charming smile changing the topic. "We have not done much today."

Then they were both immersed in their studies for half an hour.

"I will like to go now, dear."

"Ok darling. See you in the evening."

Pushpanjali was glad to observe them study happily. She started thinking about Manish. Time to time she pondered her relationship with Manish. She still did not understand whether they were only friends or loved each other. She was still engrossed in her thinking when she got call from Manish.

"Pushpanjali, I have not had coffee with you for a long time. I miss you dear."

"What a coincidence, I was also thinking about you. I miss you too. Come immediately," said Pushpanjali, eyes sparkling with utter hilarity. "Mom and daddy were also asking for you today. They wanted to meet you before we go to Calcutta."

Pradeep and Prachi were sitting in the drawing room when Manish arrived. Parinita and Pushpanjali were also sitting together on the sofa. All welcomed Manish with smile.

"How are you Manish? Where have you been shortly? I have not seen you for a long time," said Pradeep. "You appear to be very busy nowadays. Have you not delegated your work to others?"

"I have hired a suitable hand and delegated lot of work to him as you had suggested that day. Now I feel free to handle more important things and supervise in a better manner," asserted Manish. "Recently some workload has increased as I had to make all the arrangements for the Calcutta workshop. We had to arrange a venue in the Grand Hotel. I had to prepare power point presentation file for Pushpanjali. It is her first such workshop. I want that slides are self-sufficient."

"Are you sure, she can handle it adroitly?" queried Pradeep. "She is doing it first time."

"Yes, I am sure, she can handle it efficiently. I have seen her speaking and interacting adroitly. She has the requisite confidence and talent. She has also participated in such workshops earlier. I will also be there in the workshop. I will help her, if there is need," asserted Manish. "She will get an opportunity to further sharpen her tools. I wanted to discuss the program with Pushpanjali in detail, so that she is mentally prepared, before we reach Calcutta."

He started briefing Pushpanjali, "*Smile Your Way to Happiness* is 2 days program. This is, as usual, an interactive workshop. So far I have received 40 entries and I am expecting 10 more conversion from the seminar being organized by Vikas at Deegha, a marvelous beach, a tourist place near Calcutta.

Some participants have shown their willingness to join at Calcutta workshop. I will give you 'power point file' well in advance, so that you can rehearse and practice. We will discuss in detail after you go through it once."

"I am happy you are giving this opportunity to Pushpanjali. This will be great experience for her," said Prachi. "This will help her develop her personality further."

He nodded with smile.

"Thanks for very good coffee, aunty. Thank you very much uncle. Take care," said Manish. "I have to move now".

CHAPTER 16

Flight landed at 3 in the afternoon. The weather was fine and pleasant. It was cloudy and cool wind was blowing. Both were happy together. There was not much traffic and it did not take much time in the way.

"You might be tired now. Please go to your room and relax. I am also feeling stiff and want to have a short nap. We may swim in the evening together if you like. They have a beautiful swimming pool."

"I am not expert swimmer and I will not take risk."

"You are not a novice either. You know enough for this swimming pool. To be more on safer side you may avoid depth. I am also there to help you madam," said Manish smilingly. "Or is there some other reason to avoid swimming with me?"

"May be," she chuckled and smiled charmingly. "We will swim after having a nap."

"Will you like to take tea before you go to your room?"

"We had just had in the flight. Now, we will have after rest."

She reached the swimming pool and found that Manish was already waiting for her near the pool in swim suit. She went in changing room and returned. She felt that the swimming costumes alleged to be of free size were not freeing at all. She felt a bit uncomfortable in them. He looked up and caught her eyes. She lowered her gaze and acted as if she had not noticed his eyes sweeping length of her frame. Both entered in the pool. Temperature was cozy. She knew swimming, but she was still taking ample precaution.

"Why are you looking constantly at me?" quipped Pushpanjali. "It is not fair."

"No dear, do not misunderstand me. I am simply looking at beautiful soul in the well-proportioned body," said Manish laughing. "We must always be grateful to God for so many things he has given us."

"Actually I feel uncomfortable in these tight costumes," said Pushpanjali with edgy look.

"Take it easy, no one else is there in the pool now," said Manish comforting her and changed the topic. "You trained me how to dance and I will train you to be a good swimmer. It is a wholesome exercise. Now I tell you how to swim in the standing position and how to float."

"Thanks Manish," mumbled Pushpanjali joyfully. "I am eager to learn and become a good swimmer."

They passed pretty long time together in swimming pool. She readily learned various swimming techniques and practiced them with full attentiveness. She was now feeling more comfortable and was swimming on the deeper end with ease. Manish was swimming continuously near her to help her gain more self-confidence.

Both reached the conference room reserved for workshop. They checked audio-visual device and found that they were functioning perfectly. Sitting arrangement was fine. Participants had started reaching. Some of them were filling forms, some were looking at the books and CDs displayed for sale and some were taking tea and coffee.

Pushpanjali started with bright smile, "Good morning everybody. You are all welcome in this beautiful work shop. We are going to have wonderful time together. This is an interactive workshop and there should be lot of interaction. Exciting thing about the ideas is putting them to work. We have to launch them away from shore to create pattern. We have to come out of our comfort zones and plunge deep and test the strength of our ideology. You may ask any question about the topic under discussion without hesitation. Please do not start discussion among yourselves."

"Some time we have something to discuss among ourselves," cooed Mona.

"You are correct. I also want there should be more interaction and active participation. You may do it by all means, but please, involve me also in the discussions. I want that there should be minimum distraction and maximum persons should be benefited from discussion. Also, I request you to please keep your phones in the vibration mode, preferably in silent mode. If you have to talk on phone, please move out of the room."

She paused for a few seconds and said with a smile, "I will like to have brief introduction from everybody. I will also like to know what you expect from this workshop."

"Now please stand up, get introduced and shake hands with everybody and greet with smile . . .

The next step; choose a random partner and introduce each other is such a way that you are in a position to introduce your partner in front of this workshop . . . ," said Pushpanjali. She also started interacting with the participants.

Everybody was moving around and getting introduced with others. Then everybody chose a partner and asked questions.

"Now everybody will introduce his partner in front of workshop, one by one."

It was an interesting exercise and all could know each other in better way. Everybody actively participated and enjoyed this act. They introduced their partners, one by one, turn by turn.

"Having done all this, I will like to know as to what you expect from this workshop," said Pushpanjali. "Yes, Rashmi, you tell first."

"I want to apply success and happiness ideas into day-to-day living and live a balanced life," affirmed Rashmi. "I feel I am lacking something in my life."

"I hope you will get tremendous benefits from this workshop," assured Pushpanjali with confident smile. "This is a practical workshop and we will discuss how to live effectively, apply these ideas and be happy and successful."

"I want to be calm, composed, confident and relaxed and free from stress in the face of unexpected problems," asserted Shruti. "I want to have more self-esteem. I want to be a deep lake, unruffled and serene, not surface of the lake."

"You are at right place, Shruti. You will certainly be benefitted. You are a unique creation of God. The world is incomplete without you. Explore within and find your treasure and tranquility," affirmed Pushpanjali reassuringly. "Pay your undivided attention to practical exercises and practice meditations here and after. You will get enormous benefits."

"Madam, I have, earlier also, attended Law of Attraction, NLP, Sylva Ultra-mind and Louis L. Hay workshops and your workshop at Mumbai. I got immense benefits from these workshops. Now I want to learn how to organize such workshops and start my own business," said Maria. "I have a great passion to start such trainings to help people grow."

"Welcome Maria, we will help you start your venture and we will be eager to help you establish your own business. We will provide you necessary training material also. We have already helped many persons to start their own business and they are doing it successfully. Subsequently also you contact us any time for getting guidance."

"What other help you can provide?"

"We will help you arrange suitable venue for workshops, if you ever require. Trainer's training work shop, you are going to attend as a sequel to this workshop, I am sure, will be of enormous benefit to you. The business model will be explained by an expert who is coming from London."

"Now everybody, please sit down comfortably, feet squarely placed on the ground and spine erect. Take a relaxed deep breath. Inhale slowly and deeply for the count of 5, hold for the count of 3 and exhale completely for the count of 5. Listen to the air moving into your body, and feel your lungs swell. Breathe out slowly but completely through your mouth, letting the air escape on its own," she expatiated. She paused and demonstrated. "Let the abdomen rise and fall as you breathe. Keep your eyes closed."

"Continue for some time and observe, if there is any tension in any part of body. While doing it, be aware of inner body and feel energy in every part of your body. Imagine you are inhaling unconditional love, joy, happiness and peace in side and exhaling disgust, irritation, anger, jealousy out of your body with every breath," elaborated Pushpanjali. "I hope everybody is relaxed and in receptive mode. Now visualize wonderful day ahead and set intention of the day."

"How?" asked Ram.

"Smile and visualize all the good things that are going to happen to you today. Express your gratitude to Almighty in advance. You can set the tone of appreciation and awareness for the next 24 hours. Imagine, visualize and dream of brilliant day ahead and ponder how living in the present will change your life for better. Decide and plan what you are going to do, what you are going to feel, how you are going to serve."

Everybody followed her instructions religiously. There was complete silence in the room.

She continued, "Just be yourself and feel relaxation in every part of your body. If you still feel any tension in any part of body, stretch and contract that part and let it go. Come out slowly . . . I hope now everybody is relaxed . . . How do you feel now?"

"Yes, I feel great tranquility and body is relaxed." said Reena. "Senses are responding in a better manner. I feel more serene within. I have clear picture in my mind how I am going to live and feel today."

"I have clear picture how this day is going to unfold. I feel happiness and joy within and senses are responding with effortless ease," affirmed John. "I will make it a regular practice."

"I have set intention of the day. I visualized the marvelous day ahead. I expressed my gratitude to God in advance for wonderful day I am going to have," asserted Mona. "I have also decided to be kind to others and help needy persons. I will share happiness with maximum persons."

"Now I think it is a proper time to enjoy tea, coffee and delicious snacks just outside in the verdant lawn with fragrant flowers," said Pushpanjali with smile. "Let us go and enjoy the break. We will be back after 20 minutes."

CHAPTER 17

"**W**elcome back. I hope everybody is now fresh. Please clap your hands vigorously. Yes . . . great. Clapping generates lot of energy," she said clapping vigorously. "Come on, clap faster with more energy and vigor."

Everybody was clapping with vigor. Everybody enjoyed the exercise.

"Let us now express our gratitude to God. He has given us so many things; fresh air, clean water to drink, peace and happiness," she said. "Repeat with me now: '*Today, day by day, in every way, through the grace of God, I and my family members are getting better and better, more confident and healthier. With your help, God! I and my family members are free from disease, infirmities and problems. God! You have given me many blessings and amenities, which I could have less. You have made me free from problems. Thank you very much God*'."

Pushpanjali paused for the moment and continued with relaxed and pleasant demeanor, "Everybody, please write down on your writing pad, 10 things for which you are grateful to God. If you finding it difficult, just look around, there are so many things to be thankful about. You have probably fresh air to breathe, clean water to drink. You have lovely friends, family members and colleagues."

While everybody became busy writing, as she advised, she continued smiling with the brightest of smiles, "Every night before going to sleep, try to think of some happy thoughts from your day. Take time to be grateful for your partner, who is there for you through thick and thin, for your friends, who support you all the way, and for your children, who love you incessantly. Unconditional love and gratefulness creates wonderful and amiable environment in families."

"I agree with you madam. One day my 10 year old daughter hugged me and said, 'you are the best and the most wonderful mom in the entire world!' I smiled and asked, 'How do you know that? You haven't met every mom in the entire world.' My daughter hugged me tighter and said with bright smile, looking into my eyes, 'Yes, I have, because you are my world. I am grateful to you for being in my life and I am grateful to God for giving me such a wonderful mom.' I danced with joy to hear so pleasing words," said Mona. "I still relish the memory of her sweet words."

"Very good Mona; how wonderful experience!" said Pushpanjali with twinkle in her eyes. "Bless everything and everybody at the earliest opportunity. Bless your boss who keeps on believing in your work, and even the cab driver who takes you home safely. Happiness is a mixture of positive emotions, ranging from a feeling of heavenly bliss or delight to a state of well-being and contentment. Be pleased with even the minor details of your life and promptly express your gratitude."

"Express your gratitude for the drive and the motivation that keeps you going and helps you live your life every single day. Be grateful to God at every step. He is always there to help and guide us. Be in receptive mode to gracefully accept his blessing," added Manish.

"Thanks Manish," said Pushpanjali.

"Is there any connection between unconditional love and gratitude?" enquired Joseph.

"God is always with us. He never leaves us alone and helps us in every situation without any strings attached. It is his unconditional love towards us. We should be in receptive mode and acknowledge His help, as Manish has just expressed. We should be grateful to him and pass on his blessings to needy persons," Pushpanjali expatiated in detail. "Let us go deeper and discuss in detail the 'Unconditional Love'. There are so many examples of unconditional love in our daily lives. Can anybody share some example of such a love?"

"I am giving an example from my own life. One day, I got a phone call from my son's kindergarten teacher. She asked me why I wasn't providing lunch to my son over the past few days. Confused, I hung up the phone and asked my son what he was doing with his lunches. He explained, 'My friend's mom is in the hospital and is not able to prepare any meals for the last 2 weeks, so I gave a few of my lunches to her.' I was thrilled to hear these words from him," said Rashmi. "I am proud of my son. He always helps needy persons."

"It is a very good example. Please tell me some more examples."

"I used to visit a nursing home in my vicinity for helping needy people and for charity work. There I met an elderly couple. They have been married 43 years. She had a stroke and was unable to stand, eat, talk or do anything without help. He doesn't need to live in a nursing home, but he does, just to be with her and help her. Every day he eats his food, feeds her, and sits next to her looking at her like he must have, during the days they were newly married. I can never forget unconditional and undying love and loyalty they had for each other," said Sumit. "They are constant source of motivation for me and others."

"Very good; very inspiring indeed," remarked Pushpanjali. "Ramesh, do you want to share with us something."

"I used to visit a hospital for providing food and old cloth where poor people throng from slums for treatment. The boy, to whom I was giving the sweets and snacks, said that he didn't desire it. I asked the reason. He, then, pointed to his friend behind him and said, 'I want this birthday boy here to have two plates on his special day. It's the only gift I can give to him here.' His friend was elated to hear this comment. People who have nothing, also give," said Ramesh. "I felt greatly inspired to help needy persons."

"One day on my way home from work, I noticed an elderly woman with a cane, struggling to make her way down the street. As I stopped at a light, I watched a cab driver stop and say to the lady, 'I will give you a ride free of charge,' and then he helped the woman into the car," said Varun. "I was inspired to be more kind to the persons who need help."

"I returned to school with burn marks on my face and body after being hospitalized for nearly a month or so, for injuries I got in a fire. I found pink roses daily on my seat in the morning. I have no clue as to who was leaving me these roses on my seat. I sometimes arrived early to find out that great soul, but each time the roses were already there," said Ram. "Even today, I do not know who that great person was. That incident inspired me to pass on such acts of kindness to others in days to come. It gives immense pleasure to give for the joy of giving, without expecting anything from others and doing something for others without getting found out."

"There are examples galore in our day-to-day lives. Does anybody else want to share or say something? Come on. I feel, there should be more participation in interactions," said Pushpanjali. "Henry Van Dyke said, '*Use what talent you possess: the woods would be very silent, if no birds sang except those that sang best.*' So, friends participate more to make this workshop more interesting."

"My taxi driver waited at the railway station at a short distance, free of charge, in the night, with his headlights pointing in my direction, until my train arrived 20 minutes after we reached, because in his words, 'It's not safe for a young lady to be standing here at night, all alone.' He left only after train moved," said Reena. "He was very trustworthy and helpful and we hired him many times subsequently."

"Thanks everybody for sharing so many lovely examples. Now let us have a break and enjoy tea. We will be back in 10 minutes," said Pushpanjali with a smile.

"Welcome back, let us make some movements. Stand at your place. Take deep breath. Extend your left arm and let your hand hang loose from wrist.

Shake and vibrate your left hand, then do the same action with your right hand then raise legs one by one and shake. Now shake together both hands, legs without raising them, stomach, neck, whole body, fast, come on," she guided and participated. "How do you all feel now?"

"Great," said everybody laughing. Everybody was fresh and happy and joyous.

"Now I take up topic 'tough-minded dynamic optimism', but before we switchover, I want to know, if there is any question or doubt about the previous topic."

Everybody was silent and appeared to be satisfied.

"When you start a new venture, you may anticipate problems and worry about the troubles which may or may not come. Alternatively you may start with hope, courage and faith, visualizing magnificent things ahead. There is difference of attitude. You may be pessimist or optimist," said Pushpanjali. "An optimist always thinks about favorable outcome."

"But bad things are also happening. We should be prepared for them also," retorted Reena suspiciously. "We should not have ostrich mentality."

"You are correct Reena, but good things are also happening. If you expect good outcome, intervening period will be passed cheerfully. Your positive attitude will help you live effectively and purposefully in this moment. Use your will power to adhere to your optimism and do not let it fade whatever happens. Be a 'tough-minded optimist'," affirmed Pushpanjali. "If you make the best of journey, you will attract your cherished destination. Even if you do not get the coveted results, you will at least enjoy your journey."

"It means you have to be action oriented to make things happen and also keep eyes on positive outcomes. Hope for the best and visualize the best," said Reena.

"Yes, if you are a dynamic person you believe in effective action and results. You take the bull by horn. Suppose anyhow favorable outcome is not coming forth, you should be in a position to take charge of your life and by your planning, hard work and courage you should be able to make the favorable outcome happen. This is the 'tough minded dynamic optimism'," said Pushpanjali. "Now I think you all understand what I mean. Any question?"

"What other things to keep in mind to be a tough-minded dynamic optimist? If I still do not feel optimistic somehow, what should I do?" asked John.

"It is your life and you are master of your destiny. How you feel and behave is up to you. Do not let others pull your strings and take charge of your life. Behave as if you are optimist, even if you are not. Fake it until you make it. If feeling affects your behavior, behavior also affects your feelings."

"I think setting intentions, visualization and gratitude are also helpful," said Ram

"Yes Mr. Ram you are correct."

"Does anybody wants to ask any question?" asked Pushpanjali. "I think we have done enough today. Let us now stop here," said Pushpanjali after a brief pause.

Manish and Pushpanjali reached Hotel at 7.00 in the evening. She was tired. Manish asked her to go to her room and get fresh. She was tired but had great satisfaction for handling the workshop confidently. She felt better after taking a shower.

There was a ring on the intercom. Manish was on the line. "Hi Pushpi, how do you feel now?" asked Manish with concern. "You might be tired after long-drawn-out workshop."

"I am ok now, but still a bit tired," mumbled Pushpanjali softly. "You are so sweet and care so much about me."

"If I do not care for my lovely buddy, then who will?" said Manish. "You have been busy whole day. It is natural to be exhausted. You did not show there any sign of fatigue and you continued with full vigor. Can you come to my room? We will take coffee together?"

"Yes, I will feel certainly better with you Manish. I am coming in 10 minutes."

She entered the room after knocking and sat in front of him on sofa.

"Welcome dear and congratulations for adroit handling of the workshop. Your performance was excellent."

"Are you happy?"

"Very happy, indeed. May I help you to relax and feel better?"

"Let me put into practice what I learned from you in the workshop," he chuckled smiling. "I will not have better opportunity to test its efficacy. Sit down comfortably on this sofa; feet squarely touching ground and let the body go limp."

"Wow great," she said with a smile and complied sitting relaxed and letting her body go limp. "But you are yourself tired. Why do not you relax first?"

"Take deep breath and inhale deeply for count of five, hold for count of three. Exhale completely for count of five. Close your eyes and continue as long as you feel comfortable. Imagine you are inhaling relaxation, joy and serenity and exhaling stress, tension and fatigue," whispered Manish softly touching her forehead with his fingers. "Observe, if there is any tension in any part of body. Stretch the tense part and relax. Continue breathing completely. Loosen your jaws, ease your frowns and part your lips. Continue deep relaxed breathing."

Manish played, on laptop, soothing and soft music about chirping of birds in forest. She reached in the 'Alfa' pre-sleeping stage. After some time, she was asleep and she continued sleeping for 15 minutes. She looked charming in this state. Manish simply relaxed and observed the sleeping beauty. He was proud to be her friend and often thought about her whether he was with her or alone. He felt that she has become an important part of his life. He sensed that she also has the same feeling about him. He did not know when he also slept. He was woken up by soft touch of Pushpanjali's hand on his forehead. She was looking at him lovingly, smiling the most charming smile.

"How do you feel now dear?" asked Manish with bright smile. "I also slept after you started sleeping."

"Excellent, on cloud nine" said Pushpanjali. "You helped me reach seventh heaven. I am totally relaxed now."

"Seventh is okay but do not go farther dear, otherwise it will be difficult for me to bring you back here and I will lose you forever," squeaked Manish laughing loudly. "You looked like a fairy queen while sleeping. I had to use my tremendous will power not to hug you. I did not want to wake you up from deep slumber."

"Really?" she chuckled blushing. "When I woke up, I saw a glow on your face. You also looked cute and lovely."

"Such demeanor of yours turns me on," she said with wicked smile, laughing and looking into his eyes quizzically. "You are blushing. Sorry dear I had never seen you blushing earlier so I wanted to see you blushing."

"You can be so naughty!" quipped Manish laughing. "You look more captivating in this mood."

"You care so much about me, you suppressed intuitive nudge from within," she whispered with a loving voice and seductive smile. She opened her arms with charming smile. "Honey, I guess I am fully awoke now."

"Thanks dear, such a pleasant surprise," said Manish and both hugged passionately, more of an embrace. "Thank you very much dear."

"Pleasure is all mine. I feel very comfortable and safe in your arms while hugging." whispered Pushpanjali, disentangling herself softly from his hug and moving away.

"Then why you moved away."

"I was feeling uncomfortable and unsafe," she chuckled with a wicked smile.

"Sometimes I cannot understand you and your behavior darling," mumbled Manish blushing. "You are enigmatic."

"Better you do not understand it now. Time is not yet ripe. You will understand when you are grown up," she squeaked with amusement.

CHAPTER 18

"**I** think everybody is here and nobody is left behind," said Pushpanjali smiling. "Welcome back everybody. Today is the second and last day of 2 day workshop. I am switching over to a very important topic. Now let us discuss about self-esteem."

"Sorry to interfere," said Manish smiling. "Will it not be better, if we first set intention of the day and visualize great day ahead before we start."

"Yes Manish, thank you very much for reminding," said Pushpanjali with a smile. "That is a great way to start the day . . . Now close your eyes . . . and breathe slowly and completely . . . Continue till you feel completely relaxed . . . Visualize wonderful day ahead . . . Now set intention of the day."

"Self-esteem is very important for success, peace and happiness in life. People have proclivity to under estimate themselves and their strengths and feel miserable."

"Humility is also important. It is bad to boast and brag," retorted John. "Should we not be realistic and truthful?"

"You are correct . . . Be realistic and truthful, but do not underestimate your assets . . . You are marvelous creation of God. Assess your capabilities realistically and favorably. You are a born survivor. There were billions of possibilities of child being created all different from other. You are rarest of rare . . . There has, neither ever been any one like you, nor there will ever be. Bring forth your uniqueness without hiding . . . Proclaim it . . . God has given us so many powers. He gave us power to laugh, smile, imagine, visualize, plan, speak, pray, help, think, choose and feel. His helping hand is always on our heads and he never leaves us alone."

"Thank you very much. I feel greatly motivated. You made us aware how wonderful we are. But we cannot be oblivious of the fact that have so many deficiencies also in us. We are bound to feel miserable when we think about them," asserted Mona. "We will still feel guilty and miserable, if we fake what you do not have."

"As I said earlier, be realistic and make true assessment. Recognize your strengths you already have," said Pushpanjali. "May be, what you consider your deficiency, may be your strength. May be, you have not tested your strengths yet. Believe that you have so many strengths, which you consider you deficiencies. I repeat, accept and appreciate your uniqueness and rarity. Explore within and recognize your strengths. You have so many assets and you are better than what you think. *A farmer found a derelict eagle's nest. There was a warm egg in it. He took the egg and laid it in the nest of one of his hens. The egg hatched and the baby eagle grew up along with the other chickens. It pecked about the farmyard, scrabbling for grain. It spent its life within the yard and rarely looked up. When it was very old, one day it lifted up its head and saw above a wonderful sight. An eagle was soaring high in the sky. Looking at it, the old creature sighed and said to itself, 'If only I'd been born an eagle.'* He did not recognize his strength which was there."

"Very good story," said Mona. "What about the second part of my question?"

"Why should you have deficiency thoughts all the time? Even if you notice some deficiency, do something positive about that. Take corrective action and be grateful to God for so many other things you have."

"Miserable thoughts still creep in our minds" affirmed Mona. "God has not given us everything we need."

"Observe and block such thoughts. Use your will power. Be proactive and take charge of your life. It is your life and you are responsible for what you think and feel," said Pushpanjali. "If you are miserable, it is not because of God. May be, it is because of your negative choices. Readjust your attitude. Choose positive thoughts over negative thoughts."

"Which positive thoughts are helpful for improving self-esteem?" asked Ram.

"All negative thoughts make us miserable. Choose unconditional love over hate, creation over destruction, pray over curse, praise over gossip, perseverance over quitting and action over procrastination. Do more than you are paid for and go extra mile. If you do more, you will sharpen your tools further."

"Great suggestion, what else I should do?" asked Reena. "What should we do, if we are faced with the difficult situation?"

"I am telling you an exercise for greater self-esteem. Sit comfortably, spine erect and feet squarely on the ground. Close your eyes and practice deep breathing. Relax all parts of body. Imagine you are totally relaxed and calm. You are light and drifting like clouds in the sky. Position yourself where you can see all the planets and stars. Imagine a scintillating star emitting blue white light. It enters your body and overwhelms you and you become a bright star. You become now very powerful and you can handle any situation and you cannot fail. Imagine you float around and visit any planet where your help is needed. You go there with effortless ease and solve their problems. Keep floating, be yourself and remain calm and composed."

"Now imagine difficult situation you are going to face. Imagine small, dull and black and white picture of depressed you and big colorful bright picture of yourself when you felt happy and terrific. Imagine bright picture shrinks into a bright pink dot. Put the sparkling dot between the eyes of black and white photo and imagine it expands and overwhelms the dull photo and it says, 'I am marvelous and I feel wonderful now.'"

"Thanks, you have explained beautifully," said Mona appreciating. "I am feeling tremendous self-esteem and I am feeling great within."

"Now I think we require some change, otherwise dullness will creep in. Please stand up, everybody. Choose a partner randomly and hug each other and continue the hug for three minutes and let the ideas flow in with effortless ease. Keep your eyes closed."

Everybody followed her instructions and there was a silence in the room. Manish was standing slightly away from group so was left alone. He inched towards Pushpanjali and hugged her.

"How did you feel Roma," asked Pushpanjali.

"I feel great serenity within."

"Did this activity remind you something?"

"It reminded me the situation when my brother went to Paris. I still remember the agony of parting with loving brother. That day I had hugged him for 5 minutes. Same feeling emerged today. Now I feel peace within." said Roma wiping her eyes.

"Everybody please tell your experiences."

"It is great feeling of loving hug. I felt great. I got such a hug long before from my father who was in a hospital," said Ramesh. "I realized that we should hug more often. I do not know why we Indians are having so many inhibitions."

"Manish, do you want to tell us your feelings?" asked Pushpanjali smiling."

"Hug from loved ones is always soothing. This is a wonderful way to express love. Both feel loving and loved. It is a much neglected behavior and we require more of it. Touch and love are emotional requirements for growth. This hug reminded me a loving hug from my cousin who was going to hostel."

"Let us now discuss about anger. We all get angry time to time and it is a completely normal behavior and many times useful."

"It means it is a good emotion," quipped Mona.

"It is a natural and a healthy human emotion and it is useful, only if it is properly channelized," said Pushpanjali. "It creates problems at work, in your personal relationships and in the overall quality of your life, only when it gets out of control. If it is not properly channelized, it robs of harmony and joy. Here is a very good quotation by Ralph Waldo Emerson, *'For every minute you remain angry, you give up sixty seconds of peace of mind'.*"

"What should we do, if we are angry?" queried Ram. "What steps we should take to get rid of it? I think bottling up anger does more harm and is worse than expressing it."

"Do not hold it, but take immediately some constructive remedial action. Gautama Buddha said, *'Holding on to anger is like grasping a hot coal with the intent of throwing it at someone else; you are the one who gets burned.'*" said Pushpanjali. "Controlling anger is a gradual process. You can, however, learn to control anger, channelize it and even master it with sincere efforts. We can certainly control anger with some positive efforts."

"What are these steps?" asked Mona curiously.

"Slow down, relax and take required controlled action, if such situation arises. Do not run away, but face the situation boldly. Some activities are very useful for controlling anger."

"Which activities?" Asked John.

"To start with, make yourself relaxed and calm. Breathe deeply and slowly and meditate. Take, one by one, tense parts of body and relax. If you feel stress in some part of your body, stretch it and let it go. Take up another such part and do the same with it. Continue breathing slowly and deeply at the same time and observe you breath. Taking 10 deep relaxing breaths can be very soothing. Walk outside and look at the sky. This will give you a calming effect," said Pushpanjali. "You may do some strenuous physical exercises like brisk walking, cycling and cleaning the house to provide a physical outlet for your emotions."

"Very good suggestion," said Reena.

"Thanks. Writing down also helps. When you are angry, take a paper and start writing how mad you are and why. What is the cause of anger? Keep writing until you feel some respite," said Pushpanjali. "Also write about what you have to be grateful for and what you appreciate about your life. You will feel serene, relaxed and controlled. With relaxed mind you can proceed to take corrective steps and prevent damage."

"How does awareness in the moment help?" asked Shabnam.

"If you are present in the moment and you are aware of your thoughts, you will notice, monitor and control them easily. If you are aware of the extent of damage, it may cause, you will try to control angry thoughts at initial stage."

"Can we totally eliminate vestiges of damage?" asked Reena.

"Yes, to a great extent but not completely. Here is a very good story. '*There was a boy who had a bad temper. His father gave him a bag of nails and told him that every time he lost his temper, he must hammer a nail into the fence. The first day the boy had driven some nails into the fence. Later as he learned to control his anger, the number of nails gradually reduced. Finally the day came when the boy did not lose his temper. He told his father about it and the father suggested that the boy now pull out one nail for each day that he was able to hold his temper. The young boy was finally able to tell his father that all the nails are removed. He said, "You have done well, my son, but look at the holes in the fence. See the extent of damage. The fence will never be the same. When you say things in anger, they leave a scar just like this one. Make sure you control your temper and avoid saying something you will regret later.'* Control your anger at the initial stage to prevent damage," said Pushpanjali. "Anybody wants to ask anything, before I switch over to other topic?"

"Now I take up a very important topic, 'Law of Attraction'. According to it, you attract into your life, whatever you think and feel about. You will attract your passionate desires for instant manifestation. Has anybody seen the film, 'the Secret'?" asked Pushpanjali. "It is a very inspiring film and it very clearly explains 'Law of Attraction'."

"I have seen it. It is a great motivating film," said Teena. "I watch it regularly, especially when I feel de-motivated."

"You can get anything you like, provided you desire badly enough and be crystal clear of your goals. Your dominant thoughts will find a way to manifest. You should see your goals specifically, till they become your second nature," expatiated Pushpanjali. "Decide what you want to attract in your life and write it down. Let the feelings of joy, satisfaction, fulfillment wash over you. Go about each day relaxed, confident and assured that your desire is on its way to you."

"What else should we do to attract what we want?" asked Jon.

"Do not overburden yourself. Delegate efficiently what you cannot do yourself. Be patient and do not let motivation fade. Imagine that you already have what you want. If you want to succeed at something, draw up a plan of action. List what you want to achieve, what you must do to achieve your goals. Spell out how you are going to evaluate accomplishment at each step along the way. If you can't achieve your goals without the help of others, pick the best people possible to help you and listen to them when they offer advice. While monitoring progress, check off items when completed. When you've accomplished all your goals, make up another list of goals. You'll do well to re-examine your goals regularly and weed out the worthless ones."

"How gratitude and prayers are connected with law of attraction?" asked John. "Do affirmations and prayers also help us to attract what we desire."

"Yes, whatever we pray for, negative or positive, God responds and fulfills. When we affirm and pray for something, we are putting forth our passionate desire. When we passionately desire something we get it. Law of attraction always works. It is as true as law of gravity and other universal laws. When you pray for something, you have everlasting faith and infuse passion in it."

"We do not always get results of prayers, do we?" asked John.

"Express your passionate desire, pray for it and have profound faith. Be patient, when you ask anything from God, as He fulfills our prayers in His time, not ours. He, sometimes, does not fulfill our prayers and He gives us what He thinks is good for us," replied Pushpanjali convincingly.

"Well, affirmations?"

"Yes I am coming to that also. Your affirmations should be based on your passionate desires. These affirmations are to be repeated time to time, till the subconscious mind takes over. Be very careful in deciding what exactly you desire and affirm. Choose only positive ideas and affirmations. If you think about being broke, poor and lonely, that is exactly what you'll become and get. Believe in yourself and your infinite possibilities," said Pushpanjali. "Believe that you deserve and will get everything you want out of life. We attract and get what we affirm and ask for. When we have a strong desire to get or achieve something, God gives us."

She paused for a few second and said, "Now I am going to take up a very important topic for discussion."

"Please do not do it now. We have passionate desire to have tea and snacks," chuckled Manish laughing. "We need a well-deserved break."

"Sorry friends, I forgot. Yes, let us have tea and snacks outside. We will be back after 20 minutes."

"What you will like to have, tea or coffee?" asked Manish. "I will take ice tea and chilly biscuit."

"Peculiar choice. I will also try this," squeaked Pushpanjali smiling radiantly. "All choices of yours are abnormal and funny."

"You are correct. You are also my choice," retorted Manish laughing.

CHAPTER 19

"**W**elcome back. Let us start with a new topic, 'Forgiveness'. Forgive others and yourself at the earliest opportunity," said Pushpanjali. "I remember a relevant quotation by Marianne Williamson, *'The practice of forgiveness is our most important contribution to the healing of the world.'* By forgiving others you will receive tremendous peace and happiness."

"I also remember a quotation by Robert Muller, *'To forgive is the highest, most beautiful form of love. In return, you will receive untold peace and happiness.'"* said Manish.

"Thanks Manish, It is a very good quotation."

"How can I forgive someone who has made my life hell? Is forgiving not a sign of weakness? Forgiving is ok, but I do not think that one should forget," retorted Shabnam acrimoniously. "People take advantage of soft people."

"It is not a sign of weakness but inner strength. Mahatma Gandhi said, *'The weak can never forgive. Forgiveness is the attribute of the strong.'* I will tell you Shabnam, how to forgive and forget. True forgiveness cannot take place without forgetting," retorted Pushpanjali with composed demeanor. "Here is another quotation by Henry Ward Beecher: *'I can forgive, but I cannot forget, is only another way of saying, I will not forgive. Forgiveness ought to be like a cancelled note—torn in two, and burned up, so that it never can be shown against one.'* Never allow revulsion to disturb your and others life."

"You have good collection of short stories and quotations," said Mona with a smile. "It adds flavor to discussions."

"Thanks Mona."

"Suppose we face a serious situation like altercation or a gratuitous and unpleasant remark, then what should we do?" asked John. "We face so many such situations in our daily lives."

"Analyze it with a positive mental attitude, with effortless ease and with compose mind. You should immediately forgive yourself and the other person and also give that person permission to forgive you."

"It is not easy to forgive. I tried many times, but I could not forgive. Sometimes resentment is so deep, I find myself helpless. Can you tell how we can do it successfully?"

"I will tell you how you can forgive and forget, especially when resentment is deep . . . Please sit relaxed, feet squarely placed on ground and observe your breathing without altering it . . . Close your eyes . . . Observe depth, rhythm, speed, and flow of breath calmly without resistance . . . Let it be natural breathing and do not try to change it . . . Just be aware . . . If attention drifts, bring it back gently . . . Be a watcher and observer with mindfulness . . . Observe ideas freely entering your mind and leaving . . . Observe sounds and silence between the sounds. Just breathe with effortless ease . . . . Continue as long as you feel comfortable," elaborated Pushpanjali and started nature sound music, chirping of birds and wind in the forest.

"How long should I continue doing?" Mona asked.

"Continue, till you are completely relaxed."

Everybody followed her instructions.

"Repeat in your mind, '*My head, my forehead and my eyes are relaxed . . . My neck and shoulders are relaxed . . . My chest, abdomen, my heart, my lungs are relaxed . . . My legs and feet are relaxed . . . I feel energy in all parts of my body.*' Continue breathing and Keep your body relaxed."

"Now think about the person who had hurt you most, and till now, you have grudges in your mind. Imagine, he is sitting in front of you. Explain to him, how you felt then, how you feel now, and what happened during those hurtful times. After you have affirmed your outlook, let him acknowledge your pain. Watch his reaction and wait for a response. There's a good chance he will understand your point of view."

"Visualize a bright pink light is coming out of you and inundating the person with the light and love. Imagine that he is becoming stronger and more serene. Imagine that resentment against that person is coming out of you as cloud and disappearing in the air and you genuinely forgive that person. Imagine that bright light also fades, but feelings of love and serenity remain throughout the meditation. Now visualize talking with him and saying;

'*I forgive you now in this moment forever and release you mentally and spiritually. I also forgive everything connected with the matter. Now I am free and you are free. I wish you joy, peace, health, unconditional love and happiness. I release you now and all the blessings of life are yours. Peace and harmony reign supreme in our minds. You are free and I am free and feel wonderful. I forgive you completely and freely. I release you and let you go. The incident that happened between us is finished forever. I wish for you your highest good and I hold you in the light. All again is straight between us and peace be with you.'"*

Everybody repeated with Pushpanjali, some persons said it loudly and some in their minds.

She continued, "Imagine you hug him and tell that you forgave him. Really do this with all of your emotional power and release him from your troubled past and let your thoughts come back to the present. Repeat the same process for another person you want to forgive. Once you have completed this practice you will instantly feel a great sense of relief."

"Does anybody want to share his experience with us?"

"Yes Reena how do you feel? I saw teardrops caressing your eyes and falling down your cheeks."

"I recalled the situation when my uncle tortured me. First I felt disturbed, and then, as I followed your instructions I was at ease. I completely forgave him and myself. I am peaceful now. Lot of burden has been removed from my soul and I experience eternal peace within."

"Very good. You should convey this to him also when you meet him."

"You can repeat the same process for everybody, one by one, and forgiving sincerely who has ever hurt you. You can also write such an incident in detail and ceremoniously burn the paper or make a boat or put it on flowing water. Water has a purgative effect. Ann Landers said '*One of the secrets of a long and fruitful life is to forgive everybody everything before you go to bed.*' Forgiveness is for you, not for others."

"The next topic for discussion is 'How to stop worrying and live a meaningful life with joy and ecstasy'," said Pushpanjali. "Since I am going to change the topic, I will like you to ask me anything you like about the forgiveness . . . It appears everybody is satisfied . . . Let us leap ahead."

"Shabnam; you are trying to say something."

"I have a personal a problem about forgiveness," mumbled Shabnam meekly. "I feel hesitation to discuss that problem here in front of everybody."

"Okay. It will be better, if you discuss it with me in the evening. We will meet in the roof top restaurant at 7.45 in the evening."

"Okay, thanks."

CHAPTER 20

"**E**verybody wants to live life free from worries. Life is too important to be wasted on worries and trifles. You have full right to enjoy your life without feeling guilty," said Pushpanjali. "To enjoy the benefits of life, one should always be free from all the anxieties."

"How we can remain free from worries? Worries are inseparable part of life. They help us in many situations," retorted Ram. "If we do not think about worries, how can we altogether eliminate them from our lives?"

"Worry never solves a problem. It never helps anybody. So, do not worry whatever happens in life. Think of solutions, instead. They, of course, help. We have to consider corrective steps and think of remedial actions to get rid of worries and thereby get success. Once we decide the action, we should act immediately," affirmed Pushpanjali convincingly.

"Life is replete with so many worries, imaginary and real. Our precious time is wasted on resolving these worries," said Mona. "Worries make us sick and weak. Worry occurs when we find ourselves faced with a likely outcome we feel is beyond our control. Tremendous physiological and mental changes take place when we worry. It also leads to anxiety attacks, as the mind struggles to cope with the tremendous pressure and stress. But what is the systematic approach to get rid of worries?"

"Mona, you might have observed that so many worries are imaginary and they never happen. They exist only in our imagination. We waste our tremendous amount of energy fighting the phantom. Winston Churchill said, *'When I look back on all these worries I remember the story of the old man who said on his deathbed that he had a lot of trouble in his life, most of which had never happened.'*" Pushpanjali said. "We should see the problem in its true perspective. Eliminate unwanted thoughts which irritate and distract you during the day, otherwise you will be upset and lose your sleep and peace of mind."

"What are the other remedial actions?" asked John curiously. "Sometime we try, but do not get the requisite solution."

"I am coming to that . . . Writing worries down on a piece of paper is very helpful. Write down the worry thoughts, as soon as they enter your mind. De-clutter your mind to enhance its efficiency. If it is late at night and your worries are keeping you from sleeping, just get up and write down these on a piece of paper or on note book and then set it aside for the next day."

"Sometimes doubts arise whether the situations will improve or not," retorted Ram. "Everything is not in our hand."

"Yes, you are correct. We do not know what is going to happen the next moment. Being optimistic, hopeful and having faith in Almighty plays an important role in conquering worries. Look for the brighter side of things. Believe that brighter days are ahead. If winter is there, spring is not far behind. So always be hopeful," said Pushpanjali reassuringly. "Next time you feel without hope, just remind yourself that this too will inevitably and eventually pass. If you cannot change the event, you can at least control your reaction and attitude."

"Does change in attitude help?" asked Ram.

"Yes it does. You can very easily handle temporary discouraging emotions with a positive mental attitude," said Pushpanjali. "Decide to be happy today, to live with what is yours, your family, your business, your job and your luck. If you can't have what you like, maybe you can like what you have . . . Can somebody tell an instance when the change of attitude eased the situation? Mr. John you want to tell something?"

"A colleague of mine, Mr. Shyam had a great sense of humor and came to office daily in jubilant mood. His enthusiasm was always an inspiration for others to be joyful. His presence created amiable environment in the office. One day everybody noticed that he was tense and gloomy. Somebody asked, "Why are you so gloomy?" He said, "My wife is involved with a man. She is having an affair with him." Next day something unusual happened. Mr. Shyam came to office in the same jubilant mood. We asked with pleasant surprise, "What happened, why you are so happy? Has affair of your wife terminated?" He said, "No, but change of my attitude helped me a lot." We said laughing, "Strange, how change in attitude can help? Are you kidding?" He said with a smile and sigh of relief, "Earlier, I was worried for her affair. I thought the she was my wife and having an affair with someone else. But now I changed my attitude." . . . "How?" we asked. He said in joyful mood, "Earlier I was worried about her affair. I thought she is my wife and has an affair with someone else. But now I think she is his lover for a very long time and she is having an affair with me. Ha ha ha." We all laughed."

Everybody enjoyed and laughed with clapping.

"Thanks for interesting, relevant and funny story," said Pushpanjali laughing. "Another important step for eliminating anxiety is to be optimist and live in the present moment."

"I agree, change in attitude helps a lot. Also living in the present moment and being optimistic is very helpful. You will not be pessimistic about future, if you live in the moment," said Reena. "But how should we do that?"

"Decide to live in the day-tight compartment, up to bed time. Let God take thought for tomorrow. There are so many positive things you can do now in this moment. Just for today, be proactive, kind, cheerful, agreeable, responsive, caring, and understanding. Be your best, dress your best today. Be polite, talk softly and make others happy this moment," said Pushpanjali. "Be a tough-minded dynamic optimist. Readjust your attitude and try to find the positive in every situation, regardless of how bleak it appears."

"If something is unavoidable and is beyond our control then what should be done?" retorted Mona.

"Be a tough-minded dynamic optimist and accept the situation as it is now. Once you accept the situation with gratitude, your mind will be calm and composed. Then you can think about solutions more

151

efficiently with serene mind," explained Pushpanjali. "Sometimes one has to go through some adversity before experiencing the good times and sometimes the only option may be to go through the storm and there is no way around it. As I told you earlier, if situation is not going to change, in spite of our best efforts, accept the situation in its true form."

"Do prayers help in such situation?" enquired Teena.

"Yes, to a great extent," said Pushpanjali. "Have you read serenity prayer?"

"No. Please tell us."

"It is written by Reinhold Niebuhr. Here it is, *'God grant me the serenity to accept the things I cannot change; courage to change the things I can; and wisdom to know the difference. Living one day at a time; Enjoying one moment at a time; Accepting hardships as the pathway to peace; Taking, as He did, this sinful world as it is, not as I would have it; Trusting that He will make all things right if I surrender to His Will; That I may be reasonably happy in this life and supremely happy with Him Forever in the next. Amen.'* Recite it daily. You will feel peaceful and happy."

"Quite relevant prayer," said Shabnam.

"You may note down one more expression by Mother Goose, *'For every ailment under the sun, There is a remedy, or there is none, If there be one, try to find it; If there be none, never mind it.'* Have faith in God. Also keep in mind that everything changes all the time and believe this too shall pass."

"You suggested for writing down problems. What is use of writing and how does it help?" asked Shabnam.

"Putting your problems down on paper and knowing that they are there for you to work through later, may help you take your mind off of them while you are trying to take rest," said Pushpanjali. "Our days and nights should be free from worries. An analysis of a bad event that has happened may be done later with a relaxed mind. We can determine a correct course of action with a calm mind, as I told you earlier. We can then adroitly analyze the problem with a positive mental attitude and take corrective remedial action."

"Some time we are so engrossed in worries that we do not know what we are worrying about," chuckled John laughing. "What should be done in such a situation?"

"You should be aware of what is entering your mind. Relax and be in free flow mode. Let the ideas freely enter your mind and leave, but be aware and observe. Watch inflow and outflow of ideas. When you are aware, you will recognize the unwanted guests and regulate them. It is your life and you are responsible for what you think. Allow hope, faith, enthusiasm and solutions."

"Great . . . tell us more about other steps, which will be useful in overcoming worries," requested Shabnam.

"Keep busy studying and learning something that requires effort, thought and concentration . . . Do something good to somebody, without being found out . . . Look and manifest your best, dress satisfactorily, act courteously, criticize not at all, nor find fault with others . . . Have quiet time with yourself and enjoy what is beautiful," said

Pushpanjali. "Manish, I have always found you happy, serene, joyful, and free from worries. Can you share with us how you handle worries?"

"Happiness, usually, is experienced when there are no worries and this happens when we do something we love or achieve something we appreciate. It comes from inside, triggered by outer events. One of the best ways to keep it is by gaining inner peace through daily meditation. Meditation is the best antidote for worries."

"How meditation works and how can we use it more effectively?" asked Teena.

"We have seen in this workshop how effective it is. Meditation relaxes mind and body and focuses our energies. Meditate 20 minutes 2 times daily and see how it changes your life for better. When mind becomes more peaceful, it functions more efficiently. It becomes easier to choose the exuberance over worry. Think about solutions of problems, not about problems. Always look at the bright and positive side of every situation as Pushpanjali has aptly described," said Manish.

"Thanks Manish for lovely advice."

"Here I want to add some more points. When you are busy with positive actions, you do not have time to worry. Listen to relaxing and uplifting music and dance . . . Watch funny comedies that make you laugh . . . Devote some time to reading a few pages of an inspiring book daily . . . Pray to God in your own language . . . These will help you overcome worries to a great extent."

"Here are a few more points," said Manish. "Count your blessings not your troubles. Persevere and do not give up when faced with problems. Harriet Beecher Stowe has aptly said, *'When you get into a tight place and everything goes against you, till it seems as though you could not hang on a minute longer, never give up then, for that is just the place and time that the tide will turn.'* So, persevere and do not give up."

"Thanks again Manish," said Pushpanjali. "This is the secret of constant pleasant demeanor you maintain through thick and thin. You overcome temporary setbacks fast and regain vestiges of tranquility quickly. In day-to-day life we come face to face with so many small setbacks which disturb our peace of mind. I have read somewhere, *'average person faces around 23 small setbacks daily'*. These are not problems but small inconveniences. You can very well handle them."

"I have one more thing to add here. We are aware of these great principles, but main thing is practice. Practice whenever possible, you will get great results." said Manish.

"Our next topic is, 'Being present and living in the moment'. Any question from anybody?" said Pushpanjali. "But I will take up this topic after lunch. Let us go and have lunch together in the restaurant."

"Is everybody present here in this moment? If not, bring back your attention gently by asking yourself, 'Am I happy now, in this moment?' . . . 'What is going on in my mind?' . . . 'What this moment is lacking?' . . . Do not just think, but observe what you think. If you observe and find that you are present, you are present . . . If you observe and find that you are not present, even then you are present . . . Observing in the moment and being aware brings you in the present moment."

"What else should we do to be present?" asked Ram.

"Affirmations are very helpful. You may repeat in your mind, 'attention here and now in this moment' . . . 'I live in the day tight compartment up to bed time' . . . 'I am happy now in this moment' . . . 'Thank you God!' . . . I woke up happy, healthy and alive' . . . 'I accept the situation as it is now' . . . 'I do everything with grace, ease, lightness and effortless ease'."

"What other things we should keep in mind to live in this moment?" asked John with refreshing simplicity.

"Pass quality time with loved ones, being focused in the present moment and being really present with them. Be grateful to God for waking up alive today, capable of enjoying and working today and having shelter for the night. Bless everybody and make them smile today," said Pushpanjali. "Plan and act now, in this moment keeping long term goals in your mind. Break up big goals in the manageable smaller goals and complete them one by one being present in the moment. Accept the situations as it is now and then try improving it, working in this moment. Meditate, relax and practice deep breathing. Feel your inner body and energy field. Allow only empowering thoughts of unconditional love, faith and hope. Be present in your inner body and feel energy in every part of your body."

"What is meaning of being present in the inner body?" asked Meena. "How is it going to help us to be present in the moment?"

"Very good question Meena," said Pushpanjali. "Everybody, please sit comfortably, relaxed and keep spine straight. Take a deep diaphragmatic breath and feel the diaphragm move downward with a deep inhalation and your tummy expand to accommodate your breath. Take another breath and allow it to escape slowly, being mindful of the movement of your belly with breath."

She demonstrated and everybody followed her instructions.

"Keep your eyes closed. As you inhale, bring awareness to the eyes. Breathe out and let your eyes and surrounding muscles relax. Now bring your awareness to mouth as you inhale and relax it as you exhale. Relax lips, tongue, cheeks and nose in similar style. While inhaling, feel the muscles of neck and relax them while exhaling. You can repeat the exercise for all parts of body from head to toe, one by one. Take a deep breath and allow your body to feel the sensation of letting go of its tension. Take another deep breath and exhale slowly, again allowing the tension to leave your muscles. Allow it to go, relax completely and don't fight it."

"Do you feel relaxed and tranquil?"

Everybody nodded.

"Good. If you still feel tension in any part of body, stretch that part while inhaling and let it go while exhaling. Continue this exercise, till you feel relaxed and rejuvenated. Now feel energy in every part of your body in this moment. Continue relaxed breathing and keep eyes closed. At this point, if you find your mind is sliding back into thought about past and future, do your best to gently bring it back to the present moment. Now affirm, '*My mind is peaceful, serene, calm and composed. I am not afraid of anything in the past, in the present and in the future. God and infinite intelligence guides me and takes care of me. I accept solutions with poise and confidence. My dwelling place is in 'now'; my mind is full of inner peace and joy now in this moment.*"

CHAPTER 21

She reached the restaurant in time. Shabnam was already waiting for her. She sauntered towards her and greeted her with feeble smile. Shabnam had already chosen comfortable, quiet and solitary seats in the corner.

"Now please tell me your problem, Shabnam," said Pushpanjali smiling and looking into her eyes, as soon as she sat down in front of her comfortably.

"It relates to my relationship with my husband. He loved me very much and we lived happily together," explained Shabnam modestly, letting out a huge sigh. "Then everything changed when he became friendly with a girl in his office."

"Okay."

"She visited our house also, time to time, on one pretext or the other. I also became friendly to her. Later on I noticed something queer among them and I became suspicious of them both."

"Oh, very bad. How he could be so irresponsible?" she said with sympathy. "Trust and sacrifice are important pillars of happy married life."

"One day, on returning from market, I found them in objectionable situation. Their body language and my incessant questioning compelled them to confess everything."

"Were they not sorry for their obnoxious behavior?" she asked sympathetically.

"They said sorry and promised to be careful in future." said Shabnam. "My husband promised to be faithful to me in future and never betray again."

"I am happy, he at least confessed and repented. How is your relationship with your husband now?" asked Pushpanjali with curiously. "Where is that girl now?"

"He expresses love and says sorry again and again, but I am always suspicious and annoyed. I feel I will not be able to forgive him. Today, however, your exercise in the workshop gave me immense hope."

"And the girl?"

"She has gone out of country."

"Do you think, they are still communicating with each other?"

"I do not think there is anything between them now."

"Do the same thing I told you there in the workshop. Do it here and now. Close your eyes . . . relax . . . and take deep breath . . . Continue with your eyes closed, till you are totally relaxed."

She complied with her instructions.

"Imagine he is sitting in front of you and he is repenting for his behavior sincerely . . . You notice tear drops trickle down his cheek . . . You put your soothing hand on his shoulder and look into his wet eyes . . . Imagine bright and soothing light coming from both of you merges together and encases you both . . . Now, feel all resentment is coming out of your mind and disappearing slowly . . . You both feel peace within . . . You say, '*I forgive you, now in this moment, unconditionally, for what you had done and I* forgive myself. I release you mentally and emotionally. You are free and I am free. You are in peace and I am in peace. I love you unconditionally.' Do it sincerely. If not successful, try it again and again."

"How do you feel now?" asked Pushpanjali.

"I feel serene and wonderful," said Shabnam. "I felt deep seated vestiges of resentment evaporating. I can feel stillness within, as if enormous burden has been removed from my cognizance."

"Let the feeling of unconditional love wash over you and do not let it fade. Resentment will not survive in presence of true love. If you have faith in your beliefs, it will not be possible for you to be offended by conduct of others," said Pushpanjali softly after a brief pause. "Where is your husband now?"

"He has come here to Calcutta with me and staying with me in the hotel."

"It is a great opportunity . . . he is here with you. Tell him everything today that you have totally forgiven him . . . Sit with him and practice exercise with him also. He will also feel peaceful, as he is also eager to eliminate resentment. He has already repented for his behavior. You have both suffered enough and now you have to live a wonderful life of true love."

"Will he reciprocate the same feeling?"

"He will certainly reciprocate, because love is infectious. Even if you do not get desired response, give for the joy of giving," said Pushpanjali reassuringly. "Do not keep your feelings confined to yourself. Say 'I love you' often. When you sit together, hold his hands, hug him and enjoy closeness."

"What else?"

"Surprise him with a gift and say, 'I was thinking about you all the time'. Say 'thank you sweet heart' for little things he does for you and appreciate his looks."

"Thank you very much for your precious time and beautiful suggestions."

"It is my pleasure. I wish you both magnificent fresh start of your life. Always keep in mind that forgiveness is more important for you, than for him or for others. It will make your life delightful and peaceful. It will be win-win for both of you. You tell him frankly what you felt before the incident and after," affirmed Pushpanjali convincingly. "Also tell him what you feel now, after you have totally forgiven him. He will understand it and appreciate it. Unconditional love and forgiveness will motivate you to work at what you are for, rather than what you are against. Your relationship will be metamorphosed beyond recognition."

CHAPTER 22

"That day you mentioned about Deegha in seminar. How is that place, honey?" asked Pushpanjali curiously.

"It is a lovely place, worth a visit."

"I have heard earlier also about this place and its entrancing natural beauty," quipped Pushpanjali. "We have sufficient free time at our disposal. What about visiting that place?"

"This is a wonderful tourist place. It has an excellent beach. You will love stunning scenic beauty. I immensely like this place and love to visit this wonderful beach. I have been there once earlier," Manish quipped smiling. "It is a great honeymoon place. I will like to go to this place for honeymoon, if I am not able to go to Switzerland."

"If it is a honeymoon place, then why did you visit the place? I am sure, you are not married yet," she laughed zestfully. "Is there 'no entry' board for non-honeymoon persons?"

"No. I mean to say, it is suitable place for honeymoon. It does not mean others cannot go there," Manish said laughing loudly. "Do you want to visit the place? I will be glad to pass some time with you at that exquisite place. We have one day free."

"Yes honey. I think we should visit the place."

"Okay, done. We will go there."

"Thank you very much."

"I liked your dexterous handling of the workshop. You conducted it very efficiently," said

Manish appreciating. "Everybody was satisfied. Your efficient handling resulted in conversion of 5 participants for higher trainer's training course. I had full confidence in your competence. I found you even better than I anticipated."

"I am happy you liked my presentation in the workshop. Your presence acts like a catalyst. I manifest best when you are with me," quipped Pushpanjali looking at him lovingly. "It is not only this time, but it always happens darling."

"Thank you. I am proud of you sweetie," said Manish, smiling with appreciation. "That hugging game, wow, it was superb."

"I still relish the beautiful moments when we hugged that day in the workshop. I was ecstatic," jested Manish smiling and looking into her eyes.

"It was a great experience. Thanks for the lovely hug," quipped Pushpanjali. "But it was not soft angel hug, as I expected."

"Yes, you are correct," said Manish "I realized and was going to ease it, but . . ."

"But what?" she asked smiling.

"Your grip was more of a tight embrace. You were responding even with tighter embrace."

"Really? I do not remember," she cooed blushing profusely and lowered her glances. "I am sorry, if I hurt you with my tight grip. I hope your ribs are not broken. Anyway, it was a great experience, honeybunch."

"Wow, it sounds poetic and euphonic. You are, these days, using honey dipped words often and getting romantic day by day."

"Really? It may be effect of your proximity," quipped Pushpanjali with wicked smile. "When you are near, the romance is in the air."

She often had a desire to be with him. In the deeper recess of her mind she was all the time thinking and feeling about his company. She always vicariously enjoyed his loving embrace.

They reached at Deegha around 3, in the afternoon and checked in the hotel at the beach. It was a simple but comfortable hotel. It was a bit crowded and there was a lot of bustle. Honeymoon couples appeared jubilant and were having wonderful time together.

"Please go in your room and be fresh. There is no hurry, take your own time to relax and get ready. We will eat something and then go to beach for swimming. Is it okay darling?"

"Yes, we will meet after an hour or so," said Pushpanjali with feeble smile. She looked a bit tired. "I will like to have a short nap."

She sauntered along with easy steps towards her room.

Wind was blowing and weather was lovely when they reached the beach. They surveyed breathtaking view. Beautiful sand stretched out in front of them. They felt their spirits dance in utter ecstasy. There were so many families and couples enjoying and swimming. Children were floating on the tubes and water toys. They liked the exquisite place. They walked together hand in hand and appeared very happy together. Times to time her strands were brushing his and her cheeks. They sat together on the sand and enjoyed the stunning location.

'What a wonderful place! I found it better that I could ever imagine."

"Yes it is, this time," Manish said flashing amused glance towards her.

"What do you mean 'this time'?"

"As if you do not know. You very well know what I mean. You were not here with me, when I visited this place earlier." chuckled Manish. "Thanks you dear for coming here and sharing some beautiful moments with me. Life is great and you have made it even more beautiful."

An elderly couple was playing Frisbee. Some children were making sand castles and some were just running around energetically and having joyful time. This area was a bit less crowded. Some persons were floating on the tubes and water toys. The elderly couple was tired and sat down on the sand.

"Are you okay uncle and aunty? May I help you?"

"We are just a bit tired and relaxing to reenergize to start playing again. We come here every year and enjoy with family a lot."

"When you came here first time?" asked Pushpanjali smiling with childlike simplicity. "Was it on honeymoon uncle?"

"Yes my child. First time I visited this place on my honeymoon like you both. You will be happy to visit this place later, like us with your children. God bless you both and have a memorable time here," said the old man with a bright grin. "You will have a wonderful experience, when you visit this place next time also, after a few years with your children."

Manish looked smiling in the eyes of Pushpanjali. She blushed, but soon recovered her composure and nudged Manish to move ahead.

"Thanks uncle. Have wonderful time with your family," said Pushpanjali with a smile. She took a sigh of relief and moved ahead. "How he could misunderstand us?"

"I told you that this is place for honeymoon couples." Squeaked Manish with a wicked smile.

A few scantily dressed foreign ladies were sitting on the sand. Manish looked at them with brief furtive glances and continued walking ahead, holding hand of Pushpanjali.

"I noticed you looking at the ladies."

"Do you mind it? What does it mean Miss Psychologist? You are becoming possessive," squeaked Manish. "Do not misunderstand darling. Actually I was looking at a properly dressed lady sitting in the end."

"Very cunning," she said laughing. "I can read your face."

Both continued walking ahead, hand in hand. He stopped abruptly and turned towards her and put his hands on her shoulders. Surprised, she looked into his eyes. Before she could understand, he hugged her tight. She responded with same passion.

The atmosphere was very pleasing. Pushpanjali and Manish also hired tubes and floated on the waves. She was very happy and having memorable time with Manish. Manish was trying hard not to stare at scantily clad torso. She looked beautiful. Sea was a bit rough and there were waves washing shore continually.

"Let us go deeper and enjoy waves."

"No, do not go far away from shore. We are not very good swimmers. We do not have to take risk."

Manish advised her not go far from the shore. Both of them ventured ahead and floated deeper oblivious of ferocity of the waves. One big wave appeared and Pushpanjali was swept away from the shore.

"You are not listening Pushpi," said Manish annoyed. "It is dangerous to go deeper. See, how furious the sea is."

"It is thrilling experience," said Pushpanjali excited. "Why are you annoyed? I never found you so possessive."

"I have to return you to your parents intact."

"Is it the only reason?"

"What else could it be?"

She continued swimming and enjoying till she sensed that she was away from shore. She was no more hearing the voice of Manish. She was swimming when she realized a huge wave appeared with roaring sound. Nothing except white froth was visible. When she opened her eyes she realized that she was far away from shore and Manish was shouting and swimming towards her. She had been swept away from shore. She was shocked and shouted for help. At the same time she decided in split of second to continue swimming steadily and making efforts to continue moving towards the beach. Manish swam towards her vigorously and shouted, "Do not worry I am here. You know swimming. Take it easy. You can do it."

He caught her and slowly helped her out. She was still under the spell of shock. Some more persons floating around and on beach rushed towards them for help. In the meantime two guards had also came for help.

He hugged her. He could feel her heart beat and heavy breathing. She cuddled him.

"Sit down Pushpi and relax. There is no problem now. How do you feel?"

She started to regain vestiges of self-control.

"You took a great risk for me," said Pushpanjali. "It was my fault. I never imagined that this might happen. Sorry dear, I should have paid attention to your advice."

"Relax; I am happy you are safe," mumbled Manish with a deep sigh.

He also regained his composure. He always had immense faith in God. He was generally tranquil and unruffled in face of unexpected problems. He spread towel and helped her sit down. He expressed his gratitude to Almighty.

"Take it easy. God helped us. He is always with us and He never leaves us alone. No problem is bigger than His might."

She closed her eyes and relaxed lying down. He spread another towel on her body. She had regained semblance of composure over the situation. She was practicing deep relaxed breathing. She realized with joy that he was so much concerned for her feelings and safety. She opened her eyes and smiled with feeble smile and looked deep into his eye absorbed as humming bird deep in a flower, lapsed into calm stillness.

"What are you thinking Pushpi?"

"I will never forget your loving gesture. You are a great friend and a lovely soul," said Pushpanjali. She sounded weak and her words sounded feeble in his ears. "I remember an instance."

"Do not tell me now about any instance darling. Just relax for some time."

"I am perfectly okay now, do not you see?" she said smiling. "Nothing can happen to me when I have a amazing friend like you to look after me."

She continued lying down till she was feeling comfortable.

"Okay, now tell me about the instance, what is that?"

"A gentle man visited Chandigarh and was swimming in the lake. Water was a bit cold and cold breeze was blowing. Two ladies of Chandigarh were also swimming there in the vicinity. One lady tried to float on the back, but she lost control and was drowning. The other lady tried to help, but she was feeling helpless and shouted for help. The gentleman swam towards them and risked his life to save the life of that unknown lady."

"Great. He was a great person and very helpful indeed. Did you meet them later? Where are they now? Someday I will also like to meet them," asked Manish interestedly. "I like to meet such persons. They are great inspiration for others."

"I meet them daily. You have also met them," she chuckled with an innocent simplicity. "You can meet them again, any day you like."

"Do not tell me . . . Are you kidding . . . ? Who are they? When did I meet them?"

"They are my mother and father. This is how my father met my mother," Pushpanjali said with an alluring smile. "Later on, they came closer and married with each other."

"Wow, very romantic, a real story of unconditional love."

"Do they have same feeling of real love today?"

"After marriage also, they still love each other passionately."

"How wonderful!"

"Two years before my mother became seriously ill and dad was all the time looking after her. Most of the time, he was with her, helped her and took his meals with her. One day, we were sitting together on the bed of my mother. I asked him, "What is your greatest achievement of your life, dad?" My father turned towards mom, took her hands in his hands, looked into her eyes and then into my eyes with a smile and said, "growing old with your mom."

"Wow great!" squeaked Manish. "We must learn from them how to love unconditionally and respect each other's feelings."

"You are lucky enough to get training and specialization in real love from your parents," said Manish smiling. "The person to whom you marry will be lucky."

CHAPTER 23

She woke up hearing chirping of birds on trees in the back of his house. She loved nature and preferred to walk in the verdant lawn. While strolling in the lawn she was thinking about Manish as she had not met him for a long time. She was thinking to telephone Manish, when she heard the phone ring. To her pleasant surprise it was a call from Manish.

"Hi darling; what is going on? What are you doing nowadays?" quipped Manish.

"Hi, Manish," quipped Pushpanjali. "I was thinking about you. I miss you."

"I hope you are free now. I have been waiting for you for ages. Can we meet today?"

"Same here, honey. I also want your beautiful company. Tell me where should we meet?"

"At any romantic place, of your choice. Can we go to Sultanpur bird sanctuary? You may suggest some better place to go, if you have in your mind."

"I like your suggestion. That is a suitable place. I will like to pass plenty of time with you, as we are meeting after such a long gap. Millions of gallons of water might have gone down the Ganges since we met last," cooed Manish with joyfully. "Without you I feel like fish out of water."

"You appear to be in a romantic mood," said Pushpanjali joyfully. "How should we go there?"

"Simple . . . I will pick you up . . . We will go there by car."

When he reached her residence, she was ready and sitting with her mother and father. All greeted him with smile.

"Uncle, I want to go to Sultanpur along with Pushpanjali, if you kindly permit us."

"She has already taken my permission. She needs an outing after such continuous and strenuous studies." said Pradeep. "She studied 16 hours a day. You are both good and responsible friends. Who am I to come between you both? I have found you both immensely happy together."

"Thanks uncle for trust and confidence you have in us."

Pushpanjali looked beautiful in cream color sari with pink border, pink blouse and matching pink lipstick. She appeared more relaxed and cheerful. She realized that he was not able to remove his glances from her.

"Will you like to have tea or coffee?" asked Pushpanjali looking at him with charming smile.

"I had tea just before coming here. Now, I do not feel like taking it. Thank you very much," said Manish. "Let us move now."

"Okay, wish you happy journey," said Pradeep. "Drive carefully and have a great day."

"You look extremely beautiful," said Manish. "You are irresistible."

"Is it the reason you were looking at me constantly, oblivious of my parent's presence. They might have noticed," squeaked Pushpanjali with amusement. "How you can be so irresponsible?"

They would have been happy to notice my appreciating glances," jested Manish. "I was still careful. I stole glances, only when they were not looking at me. Stolen glances are very sweet."

"Very cunning," murmured Pushpanjali. "Now you should stop looking at me."

"Why?"

"Because road is stretched ahead, not this side. Dad told you to drive carefully, did not he?" she chuckled.

"He also wished happy journey darling and also told us to have a great day," said Manish guffawing. "I cannot imagine a great day without looking at you."

"Do not mind dear being personal, but please tell, if you ever had a crush on any girl? I mean; did you ever try to run after a girl and catch her attention?" she said looking at him and trying to read his expressions.

"To be frank, yes. I had such a feeling for a girl for one year or so," said Manish innocently. "The feeling was so mild, I did not even express it to her. Being a psychologist, you can better define that transient feeling."

"It is natural at that age. It was a normal attraction between persons of opposite sex," said Pushpanjali smiling. "What type of feelings do you have for me? Do you have a crush or you consider me a close friend?"

"I think I have both. I have extraordinary feelings, I never had before," said Manish. "I have consistent desire to talk to you, look at you, hug you . . ."

". . . enough . . . stop," she squeaked before he could complete the sentence. "Then, why did you not share with me your feelings?"

"I thought that time was not yet ripe."

"You did not also share your marriage plan," retorted Pushpanjali. "We are close friends and we should share most of our feelings. Should not we?"

"Yes, we should," said Manish. "But you also, neither asked from me, nor shared your plan. Now tell me your plan."

"You very well know honey, I had been busy with my cherished aim of getting through my Civil Service Exam. Now the exams are over and I am confident of getting through. I can now think about that issue. Nobody has so far proposed me," she said with tempting smile. "Do you have any one in your mind, who can make me happy?"

"No," said Manish with an enigmatic smile. "It is your life and you are master of your destiny. You are wonderful creation of God and there is no one like you in this world. Only you can make yourself happy not someone else."

"Do not start your philosophical dialogues, honey," she said laughing. "I am serious darling. What are your future plans for marriage? Who is that lucky girl who is going to be blessed?"

"I have also been so busy in establishing my business that I could not pay attention to this subject and think about marriage. I have, however, planned about the kids," Manish smiled a wicked smile.

"As far as I know, marriages take place earlier than arrival of kids," she laughed loudly. "Anyway what you have planned about the kids?"

"This is personal matter."

"Come on Manish, we are close friends."

"I want a son like me."

"Is it all?"

"And . . . and . . . a daughter looking like you."

"What? Are you crazy? What do you mean? Why like me? How?" Pushpanjali shot questions galore, blushing profusely, with pleasant surprise. She appeared to be extremely happy.

"Because you are so sweet and so cute. I love you darling."

"Really? You mean to say that you want to marry me. Are you proposing me?" she said with charming smile. "I cannot believe it. I am so ecstatic. I love you."

Manish was astonished, how he could say all this so easily? He paused and pondered for a moment. It was a subject which could easily disturb his usual serene and composed exterior. He looked at her askance. He was serious and pondering over what he had just said. He was happy he could say it so easily and he got desired response from Pushpanjali.

"Is it really so? Do you love me my sweetheart? Then why you did not tell me earlier?" asked Manish quizzically.

"I was also waiting for the appropriate moment," said Pushpanjali. "See how beautiful is the lake full of lotuses and beautiful birds. Let us get down here for some time and stroll around the lake."

"Okay."

"Manish, I think we both knew that we are more than close friends. Look into my eyes, not sideways," said Pushpanjali, looking deep into his eyes. She put her arms around his neck and nestled her head on his chest. He raised her chin, so that she was looking into his eyes. Pushpanjali was no longer able to resist the charm of his constant gaze, her eyes lowered and then rose slowly to his. Her face became pink; but she did not turn away her eyes, and continued to look into his, leaving her bearing wholly transformed. It was clear to her, while constantly looking through his eyes, which in that moment were truly windows of his soul, that she loved him and said, "I knew that you love me and you very well know that I love you."

"I love you Pushpanjali," he repeated and hugged her with more of a tight embrace.

"I love you too Manish," she responded with tighter hug. "You are irresistible. I, so passionately love you, that I cannot imagine living without you."

"Thank you but what is so special in me dear?" he said. "When did you realize such a feeling about me dear? When did it start?"

"It started when I met you for the first time. You can say that this was love at first sight . . . second sight . . . third sight . . . I felt it grow to maturity and leap ahead with time. I was captivated by your personality, your well sculpted face, your big eyes of an innocent child screaming for attention and your helpful attitude."

"Thanks honey."

"Manish, I have generally found you relaxed, calm, peaceful and happy even in adverse situations. You are like a deep lake, unruffled and placid," she remarked with appreciation. "Can you tell me, what is secret behind your unruffled serenity? This

177

personality trait of yours is very impressive and through this trait you entered my heart."

"It is an established fact that our health is effected by the degree of composure and contentment we feel within. If we have positive mental attitude, we have less stress and more happiness. It is our life and we should be responsible for what we allow to enter our mind. We are master of our destiny and we should be in full control of our thoughts, feelings and actions."

"I agree with you darling. The happier we are, the healthier we become. If we are happy, we are free from stress. Then we are better able to cope with mental, emotional and physical health problems."

"You are correct. I agree dear," affirmed Manish. "The more we can avoid a stressful life and live happily, the more disease defiant we become. Even if we go through turbulent times, we should remain free from worry. We should think of solutions and believe that bad times will eventually pass."

"You are correct," said Pushpanjali. "Problems do crop up occasionally and we have to pass through turbulent times. Positive mental attitude and solution oriented approach helps a lot."

"Problems are also useful, as they help us grow. If we solve the glitches with a positive mental attitude we become stronger to face bigger problems of life. Thus the more problems we encounter, stronger we become after solving these problems with determination and faith. Almighty gives us problems to make us stronger," affirmed Manish convincingly.

"I have found you happy and serene most of the time. You are like an unspoiled child who does not require much to be happy," said Pushpanjali with a childlike simplicity. "I will like to pass on this trait to my kids also."

". . . our kids . . . not my . . ." He squeaked with joy. "You do not require special occasions for remaining joyful. Happiness and joy are in simple things. Accept the situations in their true forms, as they are and make the best of every situation. The most beautiful days of my life are simple days. I know how to make everyday a beautiful day, by making the best of every moment of the day, living in the present moment."

"May I have the glimpse of the typical, simple and an excellent day you enjoyed very much? Was it some special occasion?" queried Pushpanjali inquisitively. She appeared very much fascinated. "There must have been some gorgeous girlfriend with you that time."

"No, darling. Are you crazy? You are my first real girlfriend, may be last too," he chuckled laughing loudly and ceaselessly. "I have not even kissed a girl so far, not even my best girlfriend, Pushpanjali. Even you did not take an initiative for that."

"Listen darling, first kiss is not a simple thing. In my opinion, it is one of the most splendid moments of life. It is a euphoric cloud burst moment. It erupts like a volcano from inside. If it happens on cue its importance diminishes. This happens, when you least expect it," articulated Pushpanjali with a composed voice. "And it is worth a wait that you will soon realize. The eruption of built up passion will transport you to seventh heaven on cloud nine . . . ninety nine."

"Wow, you have a great philosophy of kiss. You seem to have done lot of research on this subject. You elucidated it so clearly, I was transported to the cloud nine. I vicariously enjoyed every moment. I like it dear," said Manish smiling with a deep sigh. "Let me come back from cloud nine to the present moment . . . I had decided to pass that typical day in advance and made some preparation also for this day. Not comprehensive planning, but just awareness and simple planning."

"Where did you pass that day?"

"I am coming to that. I passed that day alone in a park beyond the disturbances of city life, where I could be alone and totally with myself and with God. It was an exotic natural heaven."

"Wow, great."

"I reached there by car early in the morning with my favorite books, painting accessories and I-Pad. In the way I listened to my motivational audios, 'Power of Now'. I switched off my Mobile for the whole day."

"Okay, go on," she said. She was curious to know in detail.

"I started with expressing my gratitude to Almighty. For a few minutes I talked to God in my own simple language. First of all I sat down on the grass and inhaled clean air. While inhaling I visualized His blessings entering my inner body. I exhaled tension, stress and misery. I inhaled love, joy and calmness. I reached no thought stage and relaxed. When thoughts drifted I gently brought back my attention in the present moment."

"I can vicariously enjoy it."

"Then I set intention of the day and visualized magnificent day ahead. I thought about God and expressed my gratitude to him for giving me so much. I continued meditating for a long time, more that I usually do. I continued till I reached in Alfa stage. I practiced no mind and thoughtless stage."

"It is difficult," said Pushpanjali. "I have noticed that undesirable thoughts also creep in unnoticed. What you do when attention drifts?"

"Yes, it is difficult but possible. I have to restart when attention drifts. I have to gently bring back my attention in the moment. With practice it becomes easier. Now I successfully do it often."

"After this?"

"I continued to be totally with myself in this stage, and then I allowed my mind to drift as an observer of my thoughts. I watched the ideas entering and leaving mind. I looked around for some time and without deliberately thinking about anything with effortless ease. I counted my blessings and expressed my gratitude to God for countless blessings."

"I can feel it. I wish I had observed you that day."

"After this I did walking meditation for some time. I walked slowly and thanked God at every step for everything He has done for me. I felt and relished blessing He has given me. I talked with Him in my own language. Then I went to restaurant and took hot coffee beside the lake watching ducks and lotuses. I set intentions of the day and visualized great day ahead. I thanked Almighty in advance for joyful events I visualized."

"You had a great day. It does not require much to be happy. We have more than enough to be happy any time," said Pushpanjali. "What else you did?"

"It is an attitude which matters most," elaborated Manish. "I deliberately kept my attitude positive by monitoring my thoughts. I had motivational books of my choice with me. I passed time reading my favorite highlighted passages. Then painted the ambience and enjoyed every moment. Painting is my hobby, but I do not get much time to enjoy it."

"Continue."

"I listened to my favorite music and sang the songs of my choice, as if nobody was listening. I danced with music and had beautiful time with myself."

"Wow. I can feel the feelings you sensed."

"When you experience inner joy, release it to the universe and let the universe enrich it further. You will attract more situations which will enhance your jubilation. The law of attraction will give you more situations to generate feeling of euphoria."

"No negative feelings came to your mind?" asked Pushpanjali stunned. "Most of time so many ideas keep entering our mind."

"I observed thoughts and blocked entry of undesirable intruders. If I, sometimes, drifted, I simply and gently brought back attention in the moment. I allowed positive thoughts and feelings of abundance only and expressed gratitude to Almighty. I recalled people to only appreciate. I did not allow hate and guilt feelings. I lived fully that day in the moment, in the day tight compartment."

"I have noticed that you put great emphasis on meditation," said Pushpanjali. "Is relaxation and meditation that much important?"

"I have found that meditation, not only calms us, but also has soothing effect on our friends, family members and acquaintances," affirmed Manish. "But the most important benefit of meditation is that it works like a shield against negative influences of others. The more peaceful you become, the more easily you can deflect negative energies of people around you. People cannot bring you into their misery without your permission."

"I also realized the soothing effect of meditation when I came in your contact. I used more of it in the workshop. Thanks darling for sharing. I relished a lot."

CHAPTER 24

Manish was taking tea with Himanshu when he got a phone call from Pushpanjali.

"You appear to be busy nowadays," quipped Pushpanjali. "Where have you been for all these days? I have not received any call from you. I miss you a lot."

"I was busy with my business as usual." said Manish. "You have also not telephoned me for three days."

"Sorry sweetie," cooed Pushpanjali. "I hope you are not overburdened with your work this moment."

"Not exactly," said Manish. "Why are you asking? Is everything okay? May I help you?" asked Manish. "I am always free for you sweetheart."

"I want a favor from you. You have to devote a few hours; to be exact, around 8 hours of your busy schedule."

"I am so much captivated by you, I can do anything for you. I can even jump out of terrace for you darling," squeaked Manish guffawing. "Just mention and see it for yourself."

"Do not act funny. I am asking seriously."

"Okay, go ahead. I can easily spare that much time," mumbled Manish. "Provided you also give me your lovely company during that time."

"Not necessary. I will be, however, there when you require my presence. I want you to concentrate with her and give your undivided attention. She is passing through a crisis."

"She? Who is she, by the way? How can I help her?" asked Manish astonished.

"She is a very good friend of mine, a beautiful girl and very intelligent. Her name is Nishi. Her step father ditched her and snatched her property rights. She was in love with a boy, who was also preparing for civil services exam like her. That boy also did not come to her rescue when she was facing difficult time. He is not showing interest in her anymore and avoiding her. She was so much disturbed, she could not appear in the exam. I want you to guide her. You are a charismatic life coach and you can very well handle this predicament," said Pushpanjali. "I know you can motivate and inspire her."

"Okay," quipped Manish with alacrity. "When and where?"

"Will Sunday, 10-30 morning at garden restaurant in Centaur Hotel suit you? I will pick you up to introduce her with you.

"Okay, I will wait for you."

He was ready when she reached his residence.

"Tea is ready," said Manish with smile. "So I am. I was waiting for you. My day passes beautifully, after I see your smiling face."

"Thanks dear. You will not be bored in company of that girl also. You are going to see another beautiful face. She is cute and has charming smile."

"Ramu bring some snacks," shouted Manish.

"Tea is enough."

"Let us go."

"When they reached, she was already there, sitting under umbrella near lake. The place was surrounded by verdant natural hedge laden with pink and red fragrant flowers."

"It is a great solitary place for this purpose," said Manish. "I like this place."

Nishi sauntered ahead and greeted both of them with alacrity and shook hands with mild smile. She had melancholic but beautiful face. She had flawless bright pink lips and eyes of an innocent child screaming for attention and love. She also had attractive milky complexion.

"Welcome Pushpanjali and . . ."

"Manish, I am Manish," quipped Manish with a cheerful smile.

"I am Nishi," said Nishi, looking at Manish with feeble smile with traces of gloominess. "I was eager to meet you. Pushpanjali is so fond of you. She talks and thinks about you all the time."

"Thanks Nishi and thanks Pushpanjali," chuckled Manish with amusement.

"I have to go a relative, who lives nearby," said Pushpanjali and stood up to go. "Have a wonderful time and discuss everything freely."

"Have a cup of tea before you go. You cannot go this way," said Nishi disapprovingly. "We are meeting after a long time."

"I have had tea with Manish. I will take tea with you in the evening when I come back to pick him up."

"We will accompany you up to car parking," said Nishi standing up.

"It is okay, I will manage it. See you in the evening," said Pushpanjali smiling and galloped ahead waving hand towards them.

He noticed that she was uncomfortable. Time to time she raised her glances and looked at Manish briefly.

"How is the life Nishi?" he asked smiling brightly in friendly voice. "Tell me about best day of your life. I am your friend and feel free to speak your mind."

"Sir . . ."

"What 'sir' . . . ? I am Manish, your friend," he affirmed reassuringly, looking into her eyes. "We should be comfortable and relaxed. Should not we?"

"Okay Manish . . . I am quite comfortable," she said meekly with a mild smile, sounding not the least bit convincing. She again lowered her glances.

"Nishi, why are you constantly looking down? Am I not good to look at?" chuckled Manish smiling and looking into her eyes. "Relax and be comfortable."

She sat comfortably and opened her hairs and took a few deep breaths. She looked even more beautiful with strands hanging and falling on her shoulders. She was looking more relaxed and tension free. She appeared curious to listen to him now and follow his further instructions.

"First sit more comfortably, spine erect and feet squarely on the ground. Close your eyes. Take a few deep breaths. Inhale for count of five, hold for count of three and then exhale completely for count of five. Continue, so long as you feel comfortable," said Manish. "When you feel relaxed, observe, if there is any tension in any part of your body," he added after a pause.

"Yes, I feel tension in eyes, legs and abdomen."

"Stretch the parts where you feel tension while inhaling and release the same while exhaling."

She continued rhythmic and relaxed breathing for some time and eased tension. Now she appeared more relaxed and peaceful.

"For some time do not allow any thought to enter your mind and reach thoughtless stage. Just be yourself, as long as you feel comfortable. Visualize yourself as a big tree, with very deep roots.

She scrupulously followed his instructions. She felt relaxed, steady, stable and firmly fixed in the ground. She felt energy in all parts of her body.

"Feel joy and energy within," explained Manish with soothing voice. "How do you feel now?"

"I feel wonderful, Manish," she chuckled smiling joyously, eyes still closed. By now she had regained vestiges of composure. "I am experiencing unlimited energy within."

"Now you look gorgeous with this captivating smile. Your smile is a great asset. Do not let it fade. Now you may open your eyes."

She smiled again, even brighter this time, looking straight into his eyes. She was feeling confident, comfortable and at ease.

"Now I feel very light, as if floating in the sky. I am serene, relaxed and joyful."

"There are so many benefits of deep relaxation. When you are relaxed, your senses work and respond more efficiently. Your concentration also improves tremendously. Now tell me about the best moment you experienced in your life."

"I had many beautiful moments."

"Recall and keep in your mind five such instances, but tell me about the single best moment now."

"It was with Prem in a resort. He was also Civil Service aspirant. We had great time together. That day he proposed me."

"Can you vividly recall the situation? How you felt, behaved, laughed and reacted."

"Yes," she said smiling.

"Can you order the same feeling again?"

"Yes, any time," said Nishi with a sigh. "But the memory of what happened later, hurts. Then I feel miserable," she added after a pause.

"You should never feel miserable in life, whatever happens. Take charge of your feelings," commiserated Manish. It is your life. You should never allow others to make you feel dejected."

"How did others hurt you? Tell me in detail."

"I tell you how everything started," elaborated Nishi. "My step brother and step father connived to deprive me of financial security. They discouraged me taking interest in business. I was anxious and upset. This adversely affected my studies. I could not appear in the exam due to lack of preparation. At this juncture I needed love and compassion from Prem."

"Did he come forward to help you?"

"No, instead, he avoided me. I tried to talk to him to bring back into relationship, but nothing worked. Then, he started rejecting my calls. I tried someone else's mobile also, but he disconnected every time I said 'hello'," explained Nishi despondently. "He feels that I am not in a position to clear the Civil Service entrance examination and I am no more suitable for him."

"Very irresponsible person," affirmed Manish with sympathy. "Do you still love him?"

"Love? No way. I hate him," she mumbled spitefully. "I know he has underestimated me and ditched me."

"He is an unfortunate looser. He could not recognize wonderful Nishi," affirmed Manish with sympathy. "He will repent for his mischief later."

"Pushpanjali also tried her best to convince him not to avoid me, especially when I was having terrible time, but he did not pay attention to her advice also. He has superiority complex and he considers me less important. I will show him that I am not less gifted than him and I can perform better than that moron." She uttered curse spitefully.

"Do not do it. Why should you compare yourself with him or someone else? You know, you are wonderful creation of God. You do not have to show and seek approval of others to prove your worth. You know and believe that you are marvelous and unique girl. Hating others is a negative behavior. It makes you weak. Be the best of what you are. Manifest your best to achieve your passionate desires."

"Thank you Manish. You have elevated my spirit," said Nishi. "He has hurt me a lot."

"No, it is your reaction to what he did that hurt you. Nobody else can hurt you and make you feel less important without your permission. Whatever you have attracted and got so far is over. Now you have to decide that you are not going to allow others to control your life."

"Is it possible?" asked Nishi suspiciously.

"Why not? It is your life and you are responsible for what you think and feel," said Manish. "Be bold. Change your attitude. Come out of your comfort zone. Take your own decisions. If you do not, others will take decisions for you."

"I can and will do it now," she asserted convincingly with confident smile. "Your suggestions are very inspiring. You motivated me to live my life on my own terms. You have given me so much confidence. I feel now enthusiastic, terrific and full of vigor."

"Again it is your reaction to my suggestions," said Manish laughing. "You are a masterpiece and rare creation of God. There is no one like you in this world. Enjoy that uniqueness and rarity. You do not have to pretend in order to seem more like someone else. Your life can be what you want it to be. You do not have to lie to conceal the parts of you that are not like what you see in anyone else. Do not you think your personality is different from others?"

"Yes, we all are different."

"Yes Nishi, you are meant to be different. Do not try to seek approval of others to realize your immense potential. Nowhere ever in all of history will the same things be going on in anyone's mind, soul and spirit, as are going on in yours right now," expatiated Manish. "But when you hate someone, you will hurt yourself more than him. You will feel controlled by him and feel miserable. Hate is a negative emotion and you should never harbor hate for others."

"In case I do not like somebody."

"If you do not like somebody, do not interact, orient or associate with him, but never stoop low to hate him. Change your attitude and forgive him. What you pay attention on grows, whether it is positive or negative."

"Wonderful suggestion," squeaked Nishi appreciating. "I will certainly follow your suggestions in letter and spirit."

"I have perceived that you have three persons in your life who have disturbed your life; your step father, you step brother and your boyfriend, Prem."

"Yes," said Nishi. "Most of time I was thinking about them. But now I have started changing my attitude towards them."

"Now you are on the right track. Formulate a way to alter your personal history and rewrite it fresh. Change the labels and limiting beliefs. Never feel guilty or miserable. Now you are going to be different from what you have been, what you have been taught or what has been done to you. You are connected with unlimited source. God is always with you and helping you. Do not allow past moments to spoil your present moments," articulated Manish convincingly. "I suggest you something, will you follow?"

"Yes, I will do anything you tell me. It is for my benefit."

"There is a Chinese proverb; *'if you are going to pursue revenge, you would better dig two graves.' Revenge will destroy you also*," said Manish softly. "So my dear Nishi, forgive all of them completely, one by one."

"Strange! You want me to forgive those persons who have hurt me and ruined my life," Nishi said meekly and fell silent. "I do not think it will be easy for me to do that. Bitterness is so deep in my psyche, it will take me lot of time to forgive them."

"I, very well, know and believe now that you can do it."

"You have given me enough confidence. I can try."

"You would have done earlier also, if you had ever tried. I am sure you will do it today," he affirmed reassuringly, looking into her eyes with smile. "You are up here at higher pedestal and they are down there at lower base. You are in position to forgive them now in this moment. I will tell you how you can do."

"Okay . . . please tell," muttered Nishi curiously.

"Close your eyes, Nishi. Really . . . Do it now . . . Relax and take deep breath . . . . a few times . . . . till you feel calm and composed. Now think about Prem. Imagine he is sitting in front of you . . . Explain to him . . . how you felt then . . . how you feel now . . . and what happened during those hurtful times. Let him acknowledge your pain."

She followed his instructions and did as he told her to do. He observed her changing facial expressions. Manish noticed tears caressing her eyes and then trickling down her cheeks. She continued relaxed breathing. It did not take her much time to gain vestiges of serenity.

"Visualize a bright light is coming out of you and inundating him . . . Imagine that he is becoming happier and more serene . . . Imagine that deep seated resentment against him is coming out of you as cloud and disappearing in the air and you genuinely forgive him. Now visualize talking with him and saying; '*I forgive you now in this moment forever and release you. I sincerely wish you joy, peace, health, and happiness. You are free and I am free and feel wonderful.*"

She repeated the affirmations softly as if in dreamy state. Manish put his palm softly on her forehead. First she felt tense, then stress subsided and she gained composure. She felt that the immense load has been removed from her mind.

"How do you feel?"

"I feel relieved, serene and joyful," said Nishi with composed demeanor. "I feel that heavy burden has been removed from my mind. I feel blissful."

"Repeat the same process with your brother and father," said Manish. Forgive both of them one by one.

She successfully forgave all, one by one. He watched her facial expressions and observed her body language. He guided her time to time and reminded her to continue relaxed breathing with closed eyes. She performed the exercise successfully under his supervision.

"Yes . . . I have done it . . . Thanks Manish . . ." she chuckled enthusiastically. "I feel immense load has been removed from my psyche. I am sure my life is going to be metamorphosed beyond recognition. I never imagined that I could do this. I am so much thankful to you," said Nishi with gratitude. "You are charismatic Manish."

"We are all awe-inspiring creations of Almighty, connected with same source. Recognize and appreciate your rarity dear," said Manish smiling.

"Henceforth, decide that you are not going to allow revulsion thoughts to enter your mind. You can utilize the energy saved for achieving your chief aim. Now you are going to concentrate your energies, along with emotional charge for achieving your chief aim."

"Thanks Manish . . . I was so much engrossed, I did not realize that you might be hungry. What will you like to have?" she asked with alluring smile. She appeared to be very happy and relaxed. "Let us go and have lunch. There is a good buffet."

"Okay, let us go."

"This place is famous for sea food. Do you like sea food?"

"Yes, I love it . . . especially prawn and crab."

"I also like sea food," said Nishi with enticing smile. She took fried prawns and put 2 pieces in plate of Manish. "Taste these crispy and delectable prawns. This is my favorite dish."

"Thank you, Nishi," said Manish. "Let us go and sit in the lawn outside."

"Yes, Manish. This is a quite happening place. People from all over city throng this place. This is a favorite place for romantic couples, deeply in love," said Nishi with a lovely smile. "You should come to this place with Pushpanjali someday . . . Will you like to take coffee?" she asked after a brief pause.

"We will take it at our place. Let us go there."

"Write down 10 blessing you have," said Manish, taking a few coffee sips. "God has given us so many things. We should be grateful to Him for so many blessings."

"I have never thought earlier on these lines."

"May be, this is why, it is taking pretty long time for you to write," quipped Manish. "We do not realize how blessed we are. We take so many of our blessings for granted. So many of them go unnoticed. God has given another beautiful day . . . We woke up healthy and alive . . . We have free air to breathe . . . We have fresh water to drink . . . We have so many friends and relatives, who love us a lot without any condition attached."

"Thank you. You have made me realize the blessings and abundance we enjoy without noticing. There are so many amenities to be grateful for . . . I have now written."

"Add one more point," said Manish with a bright smile, looking into her eyes. "God has given you an attractive face with a captivating smile."

"Really?" She jested blushing with alluring smile. "Thanks."

"I am not saying this just to please you. Look into mirror yourself and see how lovely and lovable you are. Make it a regular practice to appreciate what you see in the mirror and express gratitude to God. Also practice regularly to write your blessings and express your gratitude to God. Keep this list with you always. You are far better than you think. You are healthy and abundant. You have a nice-looking face with tempting smile and expressive eyes," he reiterated. "You are better than millions. You are a born survivor. You are a marvelous creation of God. Decide today that you are never going to be miserable whatever happens."

"I feel so abundant today in your company. I never realized earlier that I have so much."

Nishi was now happy and she was actively participating in conversation and interacting with enthusiasm. Eventually her desire to change and curiosity to learn was gradually overcoming her reticence. Manish experienced real happiness to put smile on her lips and motivate her out of her gloom.

"You are better than millions and you are in the process of getting more and more abundance," said Manish convincingly. "Now write down 10 passions you want to achieve in your life. Take your own time."

She started writing and continued till the list was complete.

"The list is ready."

"Compare 1st item with remaining 9 in the list, tick the passion which you desire most."

"Okay."

"Then take up 2nd and compare with remaining items except the one already ticked. This is your second passion. Continue till you decide 5 top desires. Now note down these 5 desires on a paper."

"Which is your topmost desire?"

"To clear Civil Service Exam and join Indian Foreign Service."

"That is your chief aim, okay? And which are other four?"

"These are; to go on world tour . . . to have my own BMW car . . . to be a great public speaker . . . and to write an inspirational book."

"You felt financially ditched and you wanted to participate in business activities of your family," reminded Manish.

"You inspired me to rethink and readjust the priorities. I am no more interested in business now," said Nishi with a sigh of relief. "I have to devote myself with full concentration now for achieving my chief aim."

"Great, you should not allow anything to hinder your march toward your chief aim," said Manish. "So, your chief aim is to clear Civil Service Exam and get IFS."

"Yes"

"You should now concentrate on the preparation and forget other things for one year. Other things can wait. Life is too important to be wasted on trifles. Keep yourself away from your family business. Business will distract you from your chief aim. If you keep aloof from business, your family members will be happy and you will have required time for your main passion."

"You are correct. They will even help me in coaching."

"Cooperation is always more important than confrontation. Initiate a dialogue to improve relationship. Express your unconditional love for them," said Manish. "Forget about the past and concentrate in your studies in the present. Bright future is waiting for you. You have to start fresh with faith and hope. I wish you joy, infinite and unconditional love and eternal happiness."

"Thank you Manish."

"Visualize yourself getting your chief aim and celebrate in advance. Manifest your best," said Manish. "Never feel miserable. Repeat these auto-suggestions in your mind, time to time; I am loveable and loved . . . I always get success in everything I do . . . I am intelligent and beautiful . . . I am in the process of getting abundance and achieving chief aim of my life."

"Thank you very much. You have done a great favor to me. I will never forget your enormous help. You are so supportive. I will be very glad, if I can also be of any help to you in future. Someday, I want to give you and Pushpanjali a big treat."

"Okay we all four will sit together in some resort and celebrate. Let the time come," He guffawed. "We will do it when you clear your exam, achieve your passion and meet your dream lover."

"Thank you Manish. Pushpanjali may be coming any time. Let us stroll around the lake in the meantime."

"Wonderful idea," muttered Manish and stood up. "You did not tell about your other hobbies. How do you pass your free time?" asked Manish interestedly after taking a few steps.

"Reading is my main hobby. I also like music and dance."

"You can call me any time or contact me on social media. Here is my visiting card. I have given my e-mail and Facebook ID on the card."

"Thanks Manish," mumbled Nishi. "Wow, Pushpanjali has also arrived."

"How was the day, Nishi?" asked Pushpanjali joyfully. "I hope you were not bored."

"I will never forget your kind gesture. You both have made this day wonderful and memorable," said Nishi. She could not control her euphoria and hugged both together.

CHAPTER 25

Pushpanjali could not meet Manish for many days and she was missing him a lot. She did not get any telephone call also from him. She was walking with Parinita and Himanshu in Buddha garden. Both persuaded her to accompany them to the garden.

She was incessantly thinking about him when she got telephone call from Manish.

"Hi, where are you? I miss you sweetheart. I wish you too were here with me in this pleasant weather," quipped Manish jubilantly. "I am sorry I could not call you for a few days."

"I also miss you Manish. I came to Buddha garden with Himanshu and Parinita. They also want you to come here immediately. Please come soon. Where have you been for such a long time and where are you now?"

"It is not possible to reach there. It will takes plenty of time, I will require whole day to reach there."

"Why that much time, where are you?"

"Switzerland," squeaked Manish. "I came here for NLP training for five days. Everything happened so fast, I could not discuss with you. Once I tried to contact you, but your telephone was out of reach."

"Wow, great. Have a great time," cooed Pushpanjali. "Come back soon, we will celebrate your visit to this wonderful place. You will be glad to know that I have got interview call for civil service."

"Wow, I am so thrilled. You deserved it. I am very happy to know this. I will give you tightest hug for this."

"Oh no . . . angel hug is okay, otherwise I will have to take extra calcium," she quipped laughing. "I have to take care of my ribs. How is the weather?"

"Very romantic. Everywhere couples are in tight embrace."

"Do not be silly. I am asking whether it is hot or cold there." she said laughing.

"Very cold, except me," he squeaked laughing.

"Naughty . . . I would have disconnected, if I did not love you from the core of my heart," cooed Pushpanjali laughing. "If you really feel that hot, go to your room, take cold bath and relax."

"Okay sweetie."

"Come back soon. I am waiting for you. I want you here with me at the time of interview. Your presence gives me extra confidence."

"Sure dear. I love you. Hugs."

"I love you too. Wish you wonderful stay and joyful journey."

As soon as Manish came out of wash room, telephone rang. He was happy to know that call was from Pushpanjali. He was in fact going to call her. She appeared to be very happy.

"Where are you, when can we meet?"

"What is matter, you appear to be very excited."

"Yes dear, I am on cloud nine," chuckled Pushpanjali joyfully. "I will share with you when we meet."

"I can guess the reason . . ."

"No guessing game, come immediately in coffee shop of Meridian."

"Okay dear, I am coming."

When he reached there she was already waiting for him. She was in pink sari and matching blouse and looked beautiful. Excitement was visible on her face from distance. She strode to him and greeted him warmly with a hug.

"Let us sit down first," chuckled Pushpanjali. "You will be glad to know that I have cleared Civil Service Exam."

"Wow . . . wonderful . . . I am so happy . . . I guessed it," chuckled Manish with a broad and bright smile looking into her eyes with love. "I was sure that you would clear it. Your sincere efforts and focused preparations have won you laurels. God help those who help themselves. I am proud of you my sweetheart."

Manish was very happy, but at the same time he thought that he will not get her beautiful company for pretty long time.

"What are you thinking honey? Why you became so serious?"

"I was thinking about your training period," said Manish seriously with a sigh. "You will be out of city for pretty long time. I will miss you a lot."

"I know what you feel. I also feel the same darling. I will miss you and will not get opportunities to meet you often. But do not worry honey, we will be connected through social media and telephone. We will certainly manage to meet time to time."

"Yes, you are correct," said Manish. "Have you planned about marriage?"

"Not yet. We will plan it together at our convenience. We will discuss with our parents in detail. I hope no one is going to object."

". . . and about kids?" chuckled Manish with naughty grin. "Long term goals are more important than short term goals."

"No kidding please. Do not be crazy my darling. Be serious and responsible person."

"Okay dear. I think it will be in your interest that you complete your training first and get married later on after training. In the meantime, we will have ample time to discuss with our parents and plan things."

"Very good suggestion," said Pushpanjali. "I was also thinking the same."

"What about honeymoon?"

"That happens after marriage," retorted Pushpanjali smiling. "We should plan in chronological order."

"I know darling. But we can at least plan now."

"Okay, let us go to Switzerland."

"I think Italy will be better choice," said Manish. "I have already visited Switzerland."

"May be, but not on honeymoon with me sweetie," chuckled Pushpanjali joyfully . . . Okay then we will go to both the places. First we will go to Switzerland then to Italy."

CHAPTER 26

There was a call from Manish when she was getting ready for music program. She also wanted to telephone him earlier but she was all the time surrounded by marriage guests and friends.

"Hi darling Pushpi, what is going on?" asked Manish. "No interaction, no telephones. It appears that we have not met for ages."

"It is very difficult to get time in this situation. All the time I am surrounded by guests and these naughty girls. They are trying to eavesdrop even now. They have anyhow smelled that this is call from you. My colleagues, friends and class fellows are waiting for you excitedly," chuckled Pushpanjali laughing. "They are impatient to meet the bridegroom."

"What about you?" squeaked Manish, laughing. "Are you not waiting darling?"

"May be. I do not know," chuckled Pushpanjali laughing. "You will be glad to know that Nishi is also here with her husband. She has cleared civil service exam and she is now married."

"Wow, very fast."

"She is snatching telephone. Talk to her."

"Congratulations Nishi, said Manish joyfully. "You achieved your both the cherished desires."

"Yes I did. I will never forget your suggestions. That day you drastically changed my attitude towards life."

"It is your effort. I could elicit only what was within. You recognized your hidden potential and worked sincerely for achieving what you desired. What you passionately desire and what you get is always a match."

"You are the person who triggered the metamorphosis. You helped me become entirely different individual," squeaked Nishi. "I am looking forward to see you both as husband and wife. You are a wonderful couple. I am proud of you both."

"Thanks Nishi. How are your family members? I hope you have drastically improved relationship with them by now."

"Yes, we are all very happy together now."

"Great. How is Prem?"

"I do not know. I forgot him the day I forgave him in your presence. You will be glad to know that I do not hate him anymore," quipped Nishi laughing. "Pushpanjali told me that his marks were low and he could not get class-I job. He could get only class-II job. One day he telephoned me. He apologized for his behavior and he still repents for his behavior. He felt guilty for losing me . . . Talk to Pushpanjali. She is so eager talk to you. If I continue talking to you one more minute, she will kill me."

"I am keen to see you in your bridal attire, my sweetheart," squeaked Manish. "It is difficult to wait that long. It appears that time has stood still."

"Wait sweetie, do not be so impassioned. Law of attraction works only when you have passionate desire, but desperation is counterproductive. Cannot you wait for one more day?" squeaked Pushpanjali laughing. "Have patience darling . . . These girls will not let me continue. They are nudging each other and trying to overhear us. I have to get ready for music and dance program also. Take care. Sweet dreams."

CHAPTER 27

"**W**ow, Pushpi. You look so gorgeous today. How do you manage to remain so eye-catching constantly for such a long time?" squeaked Manish with a fabulous smile. "I find it difficult to remove my glance from you."

"Who is asking you to remove? She quipped. "Are you looking at me for the first time?"

"No. But today you look very special in the bridal attire."

"You also look happy and handsome."

"Today I am really very happy. The reason being, you are sitting with me consistently and you are continuously smiling for photo shoots."

"Thanks darling . . . I am also very happy . . . I have been waiting for this beautiful occasion for pretty long time."

She shoved him to stop when some guests came and photographer started taking photographs.

"Pushpanjali, you have tremendous stamina. You have just smiled hundredth time for photograph and you are still looking fresh and cute. You are not showing any sign of fatigue."

"You also still look fresh and joyful after attending so many ceremonies."

"Yes dear, I am very happy, but my lips are tired smiling consistently and I am bored doing monotonous job."

"May I help you?" she murmured smiling at him seductively. "I can do anything to make you happy my dear. Real happiness is achieved by making others happy and putting smile on others face."

"I do not think you can do anything in this situation. You cannot even kiss me. Can you?" whispered Manish with suppressed laugh. "No doubt we are born free, but everywhere we are in chains."

""Shut up Manish . . . Do not behave like a child. You are now grown up," whispered Pushpanjali with restrained laughter. "There are people galore in this wedding reception, who are constantly watching us. Be serious. You are in reception my sweetheart. Enjoy this beautiful reception."

"Very good suggestion for you brother," quipped Himanshu, tiptoeing from behind to their surprise.

"I presume nobody wants ice-cream," Parinita said laughing. She also appeared from behind, following Himanshu.

"How can we take it on the stage?" said Pushpanjali. "Are you both eavesdropping?"

"We have to. We can learn only from elders," squeaked Himanshu guffawing. All the four laughed.

"See, how gorgeous she looks in this dress?" asked Parinita, looking at Himanshu with captivating smile.

"Marvelous, like a fairy queen," squeaked Himanshu. He put thumb tip and index finger tip together to signify that she looked fabulous.

"Take ice-cream now. You both will feel rejuvenated. I will help you both finish it quickly and nobody will even notice," whispered Parinita, laughing joyfully.

"It is good our parents have decided to arrange wedding reception party jointly. Now there are so many persons at a place and they are having wonderful time together," said Pushpanjali with butter-soft voice.

"Yes sweetie," said Manish. "It was your idea and you suggested it."

"But you persuaded successfully both the sides to hold it jointly and they agreed. Your efforts have made this idea successful."

"Two of my cousins are coming. They are beautiful charming girls. You will feel more energetic," she whispered in his ears lovingly. "They are very talkative."

"Thank you very much Manish for coming to Switzerland. I had desire to visit this place for a very long time," said Pushpanjali. "You have done so much for me. I love you darling."

"Are you happy?"

"Extremely happy! There are so many reasons to be so much delighted."

"What are they?"

"Firstly, this is my first foreign trip . . . Secondly, the trip is to my favorite destination, Switzerland . . . Thirdly, it is with you, my sweetheart . . . And fourthly, it is on honeymoon with you honey-bunch," she mumbled with a bright smile taking his hand in her hands and resting her head on his chest. "I am grateful to God for his blessings galore. I am feeling abundant today. I never imagined that so many blessings will be bestowed on me in such a short time. I am so much thankful to you for being in my life."

"I am also on the 7th heaven with you and going to land at heaven on the earth in an hour. Though I have visited this place earlier, this visit is of enormous importance. You have made this visit most beautiful event of life. We both attracted this visit. We are going to make best of it and make it a memorable event."

"Yes darling. This is perfect example of 'law of attraction'," cooed Pushpanjali. "Do you remember the day, you first time explained it to me? I had asked whether it works. You had convincingly told me that it does work and advised me to see it for myself. Today I have seen how efficiently it works."

"You are correct. The reason for getting our desires fulfilled is our passion for achieving those desires. What we badly crave and pay attention on, grows. There was another force also at work."

"What was that darling?" she asked curiously with an alluring smile.

"That is 'synchro-destiny'," said Manish, brushing softly her head with his fingers. Our passionate desires combined together to create synchro-destiny."

Flight landed early in the morning. It was still dark and light at the airport was creating beautiful patterns. Weather was very cold. Both were excited and happy together at such an exquisite place. Most of passengers appeared to be honeymoon couples. Overall ambience was very romantic. Both were tremendously happy to have come to this place for honeymoon.

Suit was already booked for them. The hotel was adjacent to the lake and there was a beautiful park in the vicinity. They checked in and found the luggage had already arrived. They were thrilled to see breathtaking view from balcony. They were captivated by white snow clad mountains stretched in front of them.

"Let us go and get fresh and sit in the balcony and have coffee. Will you like to take something else also?"

"We had enough in the flight. Only coffee is okay for the time being," said Pushpanjali. Both liked the suit. View from balcony was awe-inspiring. "It is lovely; partially frozen lake . . . snow clad mountains . . . cold breeze . . . wow . . . It is really a heaven on the earth."

". . . and lot of privacy in natural environment," muttered Manish smiling into her eyes. He hugged her with a tight embrace.

"What are you thinking dear?" she asked putting one hand on his shoulder and brushing his hairs with her fingers.

"Nothing," said Manish with feeble smile sipping hot coffee.

"Please tell me," she insisted with soft voice and came closer. "I am sure something is going on in your mind."

"I was thinking about your definition of kiss," said Manish with a grim voice. "That day you said, 'First kiss is not a simple thing . . . It is one of the best splendid moments of life . . . It is a euphoric cloud burst . . . . It erupts from inside . . . This happens when you least expect it . . . . The eruption of built up passion will transport you to seventh heaven . . . on cloud nine . . . . ninety nine."

"So, you remember my definition word by word."

"Yes, honey."

"But I am thinking about something else . . . about what you once said," she whispered in his ears sweetly. Her warm breath was pleasing in the cold weather.

"Well? . . . What is that?"

"If you passionately desire something, release it to the universe. Do not just think about it, feel it from the core of your heart," she whispered almost in the dreamy state. She came close enough and he could hear her heart beats and experience warmth of her breath. "Sit totally relaxed . . . Breathe deeply and completely . . . Close your eyes and visualize it . . . Half open your lips and visualize you are in the process of getting your cherished desire fulfilled . . . Keep your eyes closed . . . Now visualize you are having it now, this moment . . ."

"Well . . . Okay . . ." He mumbled, as if in dreams.

Before he could speak, he experienced a pair of warm lips softly caressing and exploring his lips . . . a passionate kiss . . . . he had been waiting for a long time. Both felt quiver of frenzied excitement within. He felt her feeble flame of desire grow to forest fire proportion. He responded with same fervor and both kissed each other for a long time to quell the fire. He felt that he was floating in the sky and transported to heaven, he had never gone before. He felt that it was a memorable first experience of his life.

"We have taken enough rest for 3 days. Let us go for sightseeing today. What do you think sweetheart?"

"Great idea," said Pushpanjali. "We must see important places of Switzerland, before we go to Italy."

"There is a short site seeing bus tour starting in the afternoon from this hotel. Let us go to the reception and book in advance."

Bus was passing through green lands and frozen lakes. Surroundings looked white and snow was still falling slowly. Both were happy and having best time of their life.

"How is the destination, where are we going?" asked Pushpanjali looking out of window.

"We are going to a wonderful hill resort. But see, how delightful is the journey."

"Journey is always more important than destination."

"True. We generally pass more time in journeys than at destinations. We should make the best of our journey. The weather is also magnificent. Your company has made this journey unforgettable."

"You are correct honey," chuckled Pushpanjali joyfully and hugged him turning toward him. "Enjoy journey darling and visualize exquisite destination. That will also be marvelous."

"Yes darling," jested Manish smiling and responded with tighter hug.